THE TRAIN ROCKED GENTLY THROUGH THE SUMMER NIGHT . . .

Rap did not turn his head to watch the world go past as the train churned slowly toward the north.

"You hungry?" Aunt Spicy asked, reaching for her basket.

"No, ma'm."

"You feel all right, boy?" Aunt Spicy turned to look down at him. His mouth tried to shape the words. Then they came while he listened to his own question. "Why didn't you tell me?"

"Why didn't I tell you what?"

"That whites send us to the back of the station."

Aunt Spicy sat very still for a long time; then she drew in a deep breath, put her arm around Rap, and nestled him in the crook of her elbow. . . .

"Hadley Irwin writes with humor, honesty and an understanding of the adolescent."
—*Alan Review*

I BE SOMEBODY

HADLEY IRWIN

A SIGNET BOOK

NEW AMERICAN LIBRARY

A DIVISION OF PENGUIN BOOKS USA INC.

Special thanks to Augustine and Russell Pounds
and to Gina Wynn

NAL BOOKS ARE AVAILABLE AT QUANTITY DISCOUNTS WHEN USED
TO PROMOTE PRODUCTS OR SERVICES. FOR INFORMATION PLEASE
WRITE TO PREMIUM MARKETING DIVISION, NEW AMERICAN LIBRARY,
1633 BROADWAY, NEW YORK, NEW YORK 10019.

RL 4/IL 4+

 SIGNET TRADEMARK REG. U.S. PAT. OFF. AND FOREIGN COUNTRIES
REGISTERED TRADEMARK—MARCA REGISTRADA
HECHO EN DRESDEN, TN, U.S.A.

SIGNET, SIGNET CLASSIC, MENTOR, ONYX, PLUME, MERIDIAN
and NAL BOOKS are published by New American Library, a division of
Penguin Books USA Inc., 1633 Broadway, New York, New York 10019

First Signet Printing, February, 1988

2 3 4 5 6 7 8 9 10

PRINTED IN THE UNITED STATES OF AMERICA

Because of Chuck and Gretchen

ONE

Rap heard fragments of talk every time he and Aunt Spicy walked the dusty mile into Clearview, but none of it made sense to Rap. It was Nimrod Toles who did most of the talking.

"That man! He always stirring folks up," Aunt Spicy whispered as she hurried up the post office steps.

"How about you, Spicy?" Nimrod stopped her just as she reached the door. "Things is only going to get tougher here, and you know what tough means."

"The thing is, Nimrod," Spicy said, "you talking cigars before tobacco's planted."

"I talking sense, Spicy," he insisted. "We got to move. We can't stay here. It never going to get better."

"I not too interested, Nimrod. You know that." Aunt Spicy frowned up at him. "But if it makes you feel better, I move it about in my mind." She took Rap by the arm and started into the post office. "Athabasca, you say?" she called back.

"Athabasca." Nimrod nodded, his gold tooth gleaming in the sun.

The word stuck in Rap's mind for days.

Athabasca!

By the creek that wriggled through the north timber, the word, whispered, became a poem, a song, a chant, making magic in Rap's ten-year-old mind.

Athabasca!

He shouted the word into the black of the cistern when Aunt Spicy was in the timber picking up kindling, and the word bounced off the rain water and splintered into echoes against the red bricks, "Athabasca . . . abasca . . . basca . . . asca. . . ."

"Latch up your tongue, boy. We ain't talking that word yet," Aunt Spicy scolded when she caught him under the plum tree singing:

> Mrs. Mac, Mac, Mac
> Dressed in black, black, black
> Athabasca, Athabasca
> Down her back, back, back.

"What does Athabasca mean, Aunt Spicy?" Rap gulped down the last bite of his breakfast egg.

"Nothing now. Might mean something someday. It's a supposable." Spicy moved the steaming kettle to the back of the kitchen stove. "The difference, boy, between us humans and animals is we got supposable minds and opposable thumbs. Minds is for dreaming. Thumbs is for doing. Now get to that wash basin, Rap Davis, or you'll be late for school, and Mrs. Crumpton'll be sending Cassie Mapp after you again."

Everybody in Clearview called him Rap. His name was really Anson J. Davis.

"Your Grandma Josie named you. Figured if you

was going to be somebody in this new century, you should have an important name."

He liked knowing he and the year were the same: ten years old in 1910, as if the world had begun when he was born.

He stood at the cracked wash basin making soapy clouds on the surface of the cistern water, just like the sky before a rainstorm.

"What you doing, boy? Haven't even got your hands wet yet. Supposed to be washing up for school, not lolligagging around."

He plunged his hands, wrist deep, feeling for the hard yellow cake of lye soap.

"Pay mind to your teacher today. Mrs. Crumpton say nothing wrong with your head. Just never where it's supposed to be. Like a big old jack rabbit. Never stopping long enough in one place to figure out where he's going or where he's been."

"I listen." Rap swished the soap through the water.

"You listen. Don't hear. Get bits and pieces, and nothing fits. Now get!"

When Aunt Spicy said *get*, Rap got.

He scuffed down the dirt road toward school. How come things had to fit? He could never get all those bits and pieces Aunt Spicy was talking about stuck together, like looking around now. He could see a hawk circling over head, and if he turned and looked back, he could see the timber climbing out of the valley and running up the side of Big Hill, and he knew Salt Creek lay beyond, but he couldn't see them all in one piece. It was as confusing as Mrs. Crumpton and her explorers coming across the ocean thick as flies and discovering places he could never remember. Or that Grandfather

Clause Aunt Spicy was talking to Nimrod Toles about the other day, Spicy so small, looking up at big Mr. Toles, her head just a-shaking out the words.

Maybe Grandpa Clause was another relative coming up from the south to settle with them in Oklahoma. Someone new was moving into town almost every week. Of course, if Grandfather Clause was anything like old Santa Claus, that'd be like having another Christmas right smack in the middle of spring.

Right now Aunt Spicy needn't have worried. He wasn't late for school. Cassie Mapp was at the crossroads, all dressed up in pink with bows laced in her plaited hair, waiting for him as if Mrs. Crumpton had sent her. Cassie was never late for anything. She always paid mind to Mrs. Crumpton. She never got dirty playing at recess, and because she was so good she always got to wash the blackboard on Friday and clap the erasers against the side of the schoolhouse until puffs of chalk dust covered her face like flour. Sometimes it was hard to like Cassie.

"Hey, you, Rap Davis." Cassie's voice could rip the skin right off his eardrums. "What you doing, walking alone like a roupy chicken, staring at your big old feet? Chicken hawk come down right out of the sky and . . . Swoowhee! No more Rap."

"I been thinking."

"What you thinking?"

"Important things."

"Like what?"

"Like relatives."

"What you know about relatives? Just you and

your Aunt Spicy. I got more relatives than Mrs. Crumpton's got numbers to count."

"I don't mean relatives like that. I mean relatives like Grandpa Clause."

"Grandpa Clause!"

"Everybody's talking about him coming up here to Clearview one of these days soon and how we got to be ready for him. And Nimrod Toles say when he come, Jim Crow's going to be perched on his shoulder."

Cassie stopped in the middle of the road. "Rap Davis! You so dumb! Grandfather Clause ain't a *him*. Grandfather Clause an *it*. If you'd pay attention to what folks say, you'd know what was going on. Bet you don't even know about Athabasca."

"Do too know about Athabasca."

"Bet you don't know where it is."

Mrs. Crumpton was standing in the schoolhouse door, ringing the bell so hard the clapper whirled in dizzy circles of jangles. Cassie marched on down the road and followed Mrs. Crumpton into the schoolhouse.

Rap did not move. Grandfather Clause was an IT! Athabasca a WHERE! Just another place like Wetumka or Boley or Weleetka. They were places he knew about. Dan Creek had drawn a map of Oklahoma in the dust once and showed him where they were. Maybe Dan had forgotten to tell him about Athabasca. He'd cut through the fields and follow the creek. Nobody would see him, and if Dan was home, he'd find out all about Athabasca and Grandfather Clause and Jim Crow right now and he'd show Cassie Mapp he wasn't dumb.

Like a startled jack rabbit, he spun around, dashed up the road, cut behind the church, sneaked around the edge of the graveyard, raced across Jackson's pasture and crawled under a thicket of scrub oak. He huddled, out of breath, hidden from the world, and waited for his heart to stop pounding against his eardrums. That dumb old Cassie Mapp. How come she knew something about everything?

He looked down, and there right in front of him was a long glisten in the grass, crisp as griddle cakes, delicate as frost on parsnip leaves.

"Big old rattler! You shed." Rap laughed. He reached out slowly and ran his fingers along the empty skin.

"What's it like, Mr. Snake, crawling right out of your skin? Bet you just itch so you can't stand it and you got to get out and be on your way. Big Daddy snake, you are."

Carefully he lay down beside the discarded skin and stretched full length, feet even with the tail, his ear next to where the skin ended.

"How old you be? I'm ten. I'm bigger."

He looked up through the branches. The sun was higher now, and it felt good to be in the shade. It was downright funny. He'd seen live snakes, plenty of times, and snake skins, but he'd never seen a dead snake, except for the rattler Aunt Spicy killed once with her hoe. Come to think about it, he'd never seen a dead bird either ... or a rabbit, except for the ones folks killed. Where did they go to die? What happened to them? What if they had a burying ground of their own just like the Clearview Pentecostal Baptist Church, and all those snakes and birds and rabbits got all dressed up a-singing and crying and shouting and some of them fainting with all the other animals bending over them, fanning, and saying all the time, "Praise the rabbit lord. Oh, praise the snake lord. Oh, praise the bird lord."

He lay on his back staring at the sky. Why did weeds and grass and trees grow up instead of down? Mrs. Crumpton said trees grew just as many roots as they did branches up. He didn't believe that. How could there be that much room down there for that many roots? He tried hard to imagine all the trees in Clearview turned upside down, until the sun threw spinning chips of light through the thicket, making his eyes hurt.

He crawled out from under the scrub oak and started up High Hill, the thicket cutting out the Mrs. Crumptons and Aunt Spicys of his world, singing a song he'd just made up:

Going to rise up in the morning
On that Athabasca Day
Going to rise up in the morning
Be up and on my way.

Wings flapped from the top of a hickory tree, and a flock of crows, shining blue-black, rose cawing into the sunlight.

Mrs. Crumpton had been telling about ships in school that week, all kinds of ships that explorers used: three-masters, schooners, brigantines. For some reason Mrs. Crumpton thought ships were important, but how come, in the middle of Oklahoma where there wasn't no ocean? Only thing he remembered was her talking about a crow's nest, how sailors sat up there and looked out for storms or pirates. Why would any crow want to fly clean out into the ocean to build a nest in the top of a ship? It was dumb. Crows built nests in trees. He looked up into the hickory. Maybe that Jim Crow had his nest up there.

It was hard shinnying up to the first branch. The tree was bigger around than he, but after that it was as easy as climbing the ladder in Aunt Spicy's barn. The farther up, the smaller the limbs, and when a branch bent suddenly beneath him, he settled back, straddling a fork next to the trunk.

He was so high that the early spring breeze swayed the tree as if someone were down below pushing it. The only sound was the whisper of budding leaves scratching against each other and the creak of limbs.

He'd never been so close to the sky, so high he could see way back to Clearview, beyond the schoolhouse. And over in the other direction was Aunt Spicy's farm and then the church and Reverend Sneed's house. Someone had probably climbed this very tree one time and saw the town and said, "This is sure a clear view!" and that was how the town got its name.

He was above everything except the sky. He lay back against a fork of the branch. DOWN stopped with the ground, but UP went on forever. Maybe that was what Reverend Sneed was talking about when he kept saying, "Forever and forever, amen." The sky went up even beyond the clouds . . . even beyond the sun. You sure couldn't stop a forever.

He was just thinking he'd better climb down from the tree when a man walked out of the timber. Rap did not move. He'd pretend he was a squirrel and a hunter was coming up to get him. He was safe, he knew. Big folks never looked up when they walked; they watched their feet.

He held his breath as the man walked through the trees, boots not even crackling the dead leaves, walking hands in pockets, hat pulled low over his forehead. He was a big man, broad shoulders with thick arms. At the base of the hickory, he stopped and leaned with his back against the trunk of the tree.

"Well . . . well," the man said, slowly pulling off his hat and wiping his forehead with the back of his arm. "Should have brought my gun. Grass bent. Bushes broken. Fresh meat around here somewhere. I can smell it. Had me a gun I'd shoot it, skin it, boil it. Almost taste it now." He laughed a laugh that sounded as if it had been ripped from his throat.

A shiver ran up Rap's back, all the way from his heels to his hairline. He squinted down through the leaves. The top of the man's head almost touched the lowest branch.

"Maybe," the man went on, "I just stay 'till morning. See what critter roams around out here. Better yet, I just climb this hickory and wait and see what comes along."

Rap's hands ached from clinging to the branch, and his legs tingled. He was sure if he moved the man would look up and see him.

"Or maybe . . . on the other hand, I just go fetch my gun and come back." He slapped the dust from his hat against the side of his pant leg and ran his fingers through his thick hair. "Yes, sir. That's what I do."

Something about how the man walked away, about how he set each foot exactly in front of the other, how his shoulders remained still while his

hips moved, tugged at Rap's mind like the shadow
of an old nightmare.

Rap waited until the man disappeared; then he
slid from the tree and ran toward the creek as if he
were being chased. Willow clumps drooped over
the water like arched necks of thirsty ponies, trail-
ing their waxy leaves in the stream. He sat hidden
under the willows until he was sure he was safe,
wishing all the time he were back in school.

He reached for his jackknife. Aunt Spicy said it
used to belong to his granddaddy, but it was still a
good knife. The blades were thin, worn down from
honing, the case rough and cold like tree bark in
winter and tipped at both ends with brass—real
brass. He had learned when he was little how to
make a willow whistle. His first one hadn't worked,
but Dan Creek had been patient and spent one
whole afternoon showing him how.

He chose a switch of willow as big around as his
thumb and cut through the spongy green bark and
deep into the white wood, notching and shaping.
The hardest part was slipping off the green bark
without splitting it, and the only way was to suck
on the stick until it looked as if it had been out in
a two-week rain.

He blew softly. The whistle worked.

He sat by the creek, watching the water spiders
zigzag through the tall brown cattails left over
from fall and remembered the lunch Aunt Spicy
had tucked into his jacket pocket that morning.
The fatback was thick and sweet against his teeth.
He drank from the creek although he'd been told
not to, and wondered why good things were always don'ts.

He lay back, hidden by the tall water grass,

hearing his heart beat as regular as Aunt Spicy's clock on the kitchen shelf. Hearts were funny things. Big as your fist, Mrs. Crumpton said. He'd like to see his own heart someday. They should have put hearts on the outside, like noses and ears and eyes. Stomachs on the outside would be funny too. Bones even funnier . . . or lungs . . . or. He closed his eyes against the bright sunlight and watched the dazzling red streaks fade into the velvet dark behind his eyelids.

When he woke, tree shadows laced his face.

If he were going to ask Dan Creek about that Athabasca business, he'd have to hurry. The trail up to Dan Creek's cabin made running easier.

"Anson J. Davis." Dan didn't even open his eyes, just sat, leaning his chair up against the rough logs, his felt hat pulled down over his face. Winter or summer, Dan hardly ever looked any different: plaid shirt, faded blue overalls, heavy work shoes.

"How come you know it's me when you're not even looking?" Rap sat down on the bottom step.

" 'Cause any Creek knows if someone comes scuffing up dust, talking to himself, whistling and smelling of fatback, it's Anson J. Davis."

"If you're Creek, how come you don't wear moccasins?"

"Creeks wear moccasins for tracking game. No game. Besides . . . I AM Indian. Don't have to wear anything to prove it. What are you doing down here anyway? Thought you were supposed to be in school."

"I was. Didn't stay."

"You aren't careful, you end up like me—old man sleeping in the sun."

"You ain't sleeping, Dan. You talking to me."

"Maybe I'm talking in my sleep." Dan still had not opened his eyes nor made any effort to push back his hat.

"Dan." Rap pulled at the old man's pant leg. "What's an Athabasca?"

A wasp, heavy and sluggish, settled for a moment on the back of Dan's hand, moving its wings slowly like a new butterfly. It wasn't until after the wasp flew away that Dan opened one eye.

"Apache, you say?"

"Athabasca."

"Thought that's what you said."

"I know it's a place, but I don't know where."

"Where'd you hear it?"

"Nimrod Toles was talking to Aunt Spicy about it. Cassie Mapp, she knows all about it, but I'm not going to ask her."

"Athabasca's a hole in the ground. Some holes you dig spit up water. Got a well. Another hole oozes oil. Got money. Most holes, like this Athabasca thing, are probably full of dust and you got nothing."

"Then how come everybody talking Athabasca?"

"Your people think their hole is in some place called Canada. Up north about as far as you can go. Didn't your Mrs. Crumpton teach you about the north?"

The only things Rap remembered about Mrs. Crumpton's north were reindeers, igloos, and Eskimoes who lived on fish fat—big fat fish like whales. The fattest fish he'd ever seen was the big carp one of the Smollets snagged when Salt Creek flooded last spring.

"Why you always say to me 'your people'?"

"All kinds of people. All kinds of everything. Take fish. Cat, chubs, bullheads . . . all different."

"And crawdaddies."

"Crawdaddies ain't fish. Even tribes, all different, Choctaw, Chickasaw, Cherokees, Creek, Seminole."

"Only one kind of me."

"All kinds of you too. Some of you's blacker."

"Like Cassie Mapp. She blacker than almost anybody except Reverend Sneed."

"Well, Anson J." Dan shifted in his chair. "It's like this. Everybody was made to match the land they came from. Take Oklahoma here. Red dirt. Red folks like me. Now your people come up here from down south. Land down there's all black gumbo, they tell me."

"What about white folks?"

"White folks? Come from way up north. Snow and ice just sucked the color clean out of them."

"Dan, how old's a snake if it's as long as I am tall?"

Dan pushed back his hat and opened one eye. "Boy, you got a mind that jumps around like a grasshopper in a stubble field. You talking about that snake skin up there by the bushes?"

"Yes."

"About as old as me, I expect."

"A grandaddy snake?"

"You might say a granddaddy, I suppose." Dan hunched himself up from his chair. "Think I'll go inside now . . . take a nap. And you'd better skit home before your Aunt Spicy has something more than supper waiting for you."

He raced toward home and hid until he saw Cassie Mapp and her little sister Cody and Lacey Jackson and all the Smollets coming down the road from school; then he walked home as if he'd spent the whole day sitting at his desk right in front of Mrs. Crumpton. By the time he'd fed the chickens, gathered the eggs, slopped the three pigs and fed Old Bones and her calves, Aunt Spicy was through milking and had supper on the table. He smelled the salty richness of ham hocks simmering in broth, and corn bread too.

He closed the screen door carefully and headed for the wash basin. "Smells like company," he said, not looking at Spicy.

"Too bad there ain't. You sure wearing company manners tonight. Chores done without a holler. Hands washed without a whine."

He sat down at the table. It was his favorite meal: ham, Aunt Spicy's canned green beans, corn bread and sweet potato pie.

"You pay mind to Mrs. Crumpton today?"

His fork stopped halfway to his mouth. "Paid mind," he replied, gulping down a piece of ham, barely chewed.

"You learned something then?"

The chunk of ham stuck in his throat. "Yes, ma'am."

"Itchy day, today." Spicy rested one elbow on the table and looked out the kitchen window. "Felt it in my knees and all down my legs. Had to keep talking to them. Them legs wanted to run off with me. You know the feeling?"

The green beans dangled on his fork inches from his mouth. "Yes, ma'am."

"But I said, 'Legs! plant those feet in front of that stove and get to cooking!' "

He chewed each bean carefully, eyes on his plate.

"Saw someone cutting across High Hill this morning. You wouldn't have seen him, though."

"Didn't see no man's face." He set his fork down. Not even Aunt Spicy's sweet potato pie looked tempting.

"Eat up, boy. Ain't you hungry after all that learning today?"

He tried another forkful of ham and beans. His jaws ached from chewing, and a swallow of milk churned its way down into the pit of his stomach.

"Blood's probably all rushed to your brain from the learning. Eat up, so's it'll run back down to your stomach."

If Aunt Spicy would just quit looking at him, resting her elbows on the table, holding her coffee cup in two hands, her eyes like black cinders over the rim.

"You've got to be somebody, Rap Davis. You got a head but you got no urge. Supposed to learn to talk proper like Mrs. Crumpton. Supposed to know . . . understand things I ain't even heard of yet. Why, when Clearview gets to be a real city, like Mrs. Crumpton wrote in the newspaper last week, with skyscrapers and taxi cabs and airplanes, you got to know how to do things."

He wished he were back in the hickory with the only world the sky.

Aunt Spicy slid a piece of sweet potato pie onto her plate, took a bite and chewed thoughtfully. "MMMMmmmmmm. Best pie I ever made. Think I'll make another for Sunday. Mrs. Crumpton's coming over for dinner after church. You ready for yours now?"

"Not hungry." He carefully balanced his knife and fork across his plate.

"Not hungry! My ears going bad?"

There was no place to look except at Aunt Spicy.

A trickle of sweat rolled down the middle of his back. "I . . . a . . . I . . ." His tongue was thick with the sour taste of half-chewed ham and beans. "Didn't go . . . to school . . . today."

"Sure you did, boy. Saw you leave this morning." Aunt Spicy was no longer watching him.

Maybe he could say Mrs. Crumpton sent him on an errand and he didn't get back or that Cassie told him Mrs. Crumpton was sick and there wasn't going to be any school or that man he'd seen that afternoon had bundled him right up and carried him off. But lying to Aunt Spicy never worked.

"It was my legs," he said, not raising his eyes. "They took me all the way to school. But they wouldn't walk me in. They's all itchy, Aunt Spicy, like you say."

He waited for the scolding to begin.

Spicy scooped up the last bite of pie, chewed so slowly he could almost taste its sweetness, then pushed back her plate and looked at him again. "Well, well. No school. Maybe that's how come young Rap Davis has cockleburrs in his hair, on his shirt and sticking to his stocks."

"You going to wallop me?"

The sweet potato pie was looking better and better.

"Rap, you put me in mind of an old dog my daddy had back in Louisiana. Good dog, he was, but one bad habit. Like to chase pigs." Spicy gazed out the window as if the whole thing were happening just outside in the yard. "Every time he chased them pigs, Daddy walloped him. Went on so long that after while that stupid dog'd run down, chase pigs, come back to Daddy and stand there waiting to be walloped."

"What did your daddy do to teach him?"

"Shot him, honey. Took out his gun and shot him dead! Now eat your pie!"

He thought of the man at the base of the hickory. One bite of Aunt Spicy's pie was all Rap could eat.

The next morning, Rap followed Cassie Mapp and Cody and Lacey and Mrs. Crumpton right through the schoolhouse door, all the time muttering, "Legs! Plant those feet under that desk. Get to learning. I got to be somebody."

He made it through arithmetic. Mrs. Crumpton had them cutting up circles that looked like pies. Nothing to that. He'd seen Aunt Spicy do that all his life. Punctuation had him puzzled for a while with all those commas slipping in after words and flying up in the air around the *s*'s and sometimes even hanging up there double like rabbit tracks in dirt.

Spelling was next. He didn't know why, but spelling was his favorite. Maybe it was the way the letters looked, all black and squiggly on the white page or all white and squiggly on the black board. All he had to do was picture in his mind how the letters looked and they came right out in a string of shapes—like *Mississippi*: m-i-crooked letter-crooked letter-i-crooked letter-crooked letter-i-humpback-humpback-i. Or to spell his name, *RAP*: running humpback-tepee-humpback. He was the best speller in his grade; of course there were only two others, Cassie and Lacey.

During recess, he was best IT at I Spy, too.

Bushel ree. Bushel rye.
Who all's round my base is out.

He opened his eyes and looked around. The two littlest Mapps were hiding like nervous rabbits behind their usual stump. The twins, Ima and Esther Irby, huddled behind the girls' outhouse, and Lacey Jackson crawled under the schoolhouse steps. It didn't take long to find them. The only one he couldn't spy was Cassie.

"You don't never catch Cassie," Laveda Brody hollered, giggling so hard she had to clench her knees together. "You don't never see her 'til recess over 'cause she be in the girls' place with the door locked and you can't go in there so how you going to spy her?"

"Cassie Mapp!" He pounded on the door. "You come out. You not playing fair."

Cassie waited until Mrs. Crumpton rang the bell. "Somebody told," she said, flouncing out the door. "You'd never found me."

"You cheated."

"Cheated! You played hookey yesterday. Where'd you go? Down to Creeky Dan's I bet."

"Did not."

"Did not what?"

"Did not go to Creeky Dan's."

"I don't care where you went, 'cause Mrs. Crumpton'll get you. You see."

Mrs. Crumpton got him just as he started down the school steps that afternoon.

"Anson J. Davis. I want to see you."

He never realized how small the schoolroom was with empty desks and benches crowding in on him so that he could hardly breathe. Mrs. Crumpton pointed to the front bench, and he sat down, wiping his palms against his pant legs.

She stood above him, looking at him, the silence pushing against his stomach.

"Young man," she began, her words echoing around the empty classroom. "I want to tell you a story about a boy, not too different from you, who grew up to be somebody. We learned about him in school yesterday. Frederick Douglass. You know who he was, don't you?"

"Yes, ma'am."

"Who was he, then?"

If Mrs. Crumpton was talking about him, he had to be important. Rap grabbed at the first idea that sailed past. "The first Negro president of the United States."

Mrs. Crumpton turned and walked to the back of the schoolroom, her heels clicking against the wood floor.

"No!" Her voice almost rattled the windows. "Rap Davis, Mr. Douglass was *not* president, though he might have been at some other time. Frederick Douglass was a slave who grew up with none of the fine things you have. He didn't have an Aunt Spicy to take care of him, an Aunt Spicy, who folks honor and look up to. He didn't have a nice farm like yours, nor a cow nor a chance to attend school, nor a home in a city like Clearview." She moved up the aisle toward him.

"Bet he didn't have a jackknife like mine either. Couldn't even whittle out a willow whistle or nothing, I don't suppose."

"That's not the point! He didn't care about such things. There was only one thing he wanted. He wanted to learn ... to learn to write, to read, to spell, to understand, to change the world. And he

did learn, all by himself; and helped others. He was
a credit to our race."

Little as she was, not much taller than Rap,
right then she was puffed up like a fat quail.

"He did all that and never had to go to school?"

"Anson Davis!" Her hand came down on his
knee. "I don't know how that head of yours works,
but it's got more twists in it than Salt Creek, and
furthermore, it's not half as deep." She took a big
breath. "Now listen carefully."

"Yes, ma'am."

"You've heard Reverend Sneed tell about how
God handed down the Ten Commandments to
Moses, all carved in stone?"

"Yes, ma'am."

"Well, Mr. Davis, there is an Eleventh Commandment that the Reverend never mentioned.
Do you know what it is?"

"No, ma'am."

"The Eleventh Commandment is THOU SHALL NOT
ABSENT THYSELF FROM SCHOOL! Thou shalt attend
school. Thou shalt listen in school. Thou shalt learn
in school. And the next time, you think about break-
ing that commandment, just remember GOD AND
MOSES AND REVEREND SNEED AND MRS. CRUMPTON ARE
ALL WATCHING YOU!"

Goosebumps ran up his arms, and the wooden
bench dug into the backs of his knees.

"Now . . ." She collected her books from the
desk and slapped them into a wooden holder. "You
sit right there and think. You think for ten minutes. You ask yourself, 'What did I do wrong? Why
should I not do it again?' And when you've answered all that, you think about what you should

do in the future and what will happen if you ever skip school again."

Ten minutes! He looked up at the clock, moving just his eyes. A big wood clock it was with what Mrs. Crumpton called Roman numerals on its face. That didn't make no sense—weren't no Romans around Clearview except for Keen Roman, the depot man, and he sure never came out to school.

The clock had a shiny yellow pendulum that hung down and made the minutes go away. Just swung back and forth, moving all the time, but never going nowhere.

He sure would hate to be a clock, even part of one. He'd rather be that fly up on the ceiling—going this way, that way, landing for a while and taking off again. Of course, you could get swatted or stuck on flypaper, but if you were a smart fly, you could probably see a whole lot of places and that'd be better than moving back and forth in the same old spot day after day.

He supposed flies didn't live very long, but then the clock stopped too over the weekend and didn't start again until Mrs. Crumpton wound it up on Monday morning. Yes, sir, he'd sure rather be a fly.

"Rap!"

He jumped even though her voice was softer now.

"You been thinking about what I said?"

"Yes, ma'am."

"And you'll remember what you've been thinking?"

"Yes, ma'am."

"You know that Eleventh Commandment by heart now?"

"Yes, ma'am."

"Well, then. You may go." She reached out and touched him on the shoulder. "But Rap. Before you go . . . would you have time to erase my blackboard for me and clean the erasers?"

"Yes, ma'am. I sure do." He clapped the erasers together until his hands were white with chalk, and he washed the board until his hands were clean and black again.

TWO

"**W**ell, Mr. Davis," Aunt Spicy announced the next morning, "since you've had your day off, you can just spend this Saturday helping me."

Rap's notion to spend the day fishing whirled off like an Oklahoma dust devil.

"Need some wood for the kitchen stove. Having chicken pie tomorrow for Mrs. Crumpton, and that setting hen'll take a long boil. Those rugs need a good shaking and beating. Front porch window's all streaked."

He thought once about sneaking off, but he wasn't sure there might not be a Twelfth Commandment, and with Mrs. Crumpton coming for Sunday dinner, he knew he'd better not take a chance. Maybe if he hurried through his chores there might be time for fishing, but Rap got to watching a beetle down by the woodpile, and when he was beating the rugs he made like he was a giant whopping thunder out of the clouds, and first thing he knew, it was time for dinner.

After they had eaten, Spicy had an even longer list of things for him to do that started with "Rake up the front yard" and ended with "Run down to the storm cellar and fetch another jar of green beans and some plum butter."

The storm cellar was a kind of cave dug into the far corner of the yard and humped up like a big anthill. In winter it was good sliding on a scoop shovel, and more than once, in the summer, he and Spicy had hid there when Oklahoma twisters came roaring out of the southwest. They'd huddle by the half-open door and watch the angry greenish-yellow sky twist and churn. One time the tornado came so close it plucked the feathers right off three of Spicy's chickens and left them all bare and squawking in the yard.

Always when he opened the door to the storm cellar, a musty coldness waited for him. Four stone steps led down to the dirt floor, and rustlings came from behind the wooden shelves. He knew it was probably the old bull snake that lived down there. It didn't eat anything but mice and bugs and rats. At first, even with the door open, the cellar was dark. He'd bet anything Reverend Sneed and Mrs. Crumpton would never be able to see him even if they were standing in the door and looking in. He wasn't so sure about God and Moses.

He knew the beans and plum butter were lined up against the far wall. He had spent one whole afternoon carrying them down there for Aunt Spicy, as soon as they were cool enough to handle. He felt his way into the darkness, running his fingers along the roughness of the shelves. Right there, under his hand, on a wide piece of board he could feel his name: RAP. He squatted down beside the shelf and pressed his palm against the carving in the wood. Three whole years ago, he'd carved his name there—the summer Aunt Spicy gave him his granddaddy's knife—the same summer Dan Creek explained to him about caves: "That's where we Creeks bury our kin. With them we put things that was close to them. Things they might need when their spirits go so they won't be alone."

He was little then. If he stood up now and carved his name again, anybody could see how much he'd grown.

He'd do it different, this time. This time it would be A. J. DAVIS. He took out his knife and began. It wasn't hard. The wood was soft pine, and now he could see enough in the dimness of the cave to keep the letters straight.

The "J" was tricky to carve with its curl at the bottom. Dumb old Lacey Jackson was always asking him what the *J* stood for.

"Don't stand for nothing."

"Gotta stand for something."

"Don't have to."

"Why not?"

"Just a letter."

"Everybody's got a middle name."

Lacey always gave orders and asked questions like one of Mrs. Crumpton's tests.

"Stands for Jefferson," Rap lied.

"How come you didn't tell me that in the first place?"

"Didn't want to."

The rest of Rap's name was easy except for the curling *S* at the end. His wrist ached from holding the knife. He stopped for a minute and slid down to the floor. What would it be like if someday, when he was all grown up, he'd come back here to visit and there'd be another boy or girl who'd come running up to him and ask, "Who's name that down in the cave?" He'd just stand there and look and say, "Why, that's somebody. Somebody real important. That be His Honor Anson J. Davis."

In the cave he could be anybody: Christopher Columbus, Abraham Lincoln, Frederick Douglass. Or he could be somebody who had never been before. One thing for sure, he'd not only be somebody but he'd be big, bigger than that man he's seen from the top of the hickory. He'd be smart, too. Smarter than Mrs. Crumpton and he'd know everything that was in any book that was ever written. He'd be so smart, he'd run for county supervisor like Nimrod Toles, only he'd be elected.

Rap wondered what his own mama would have named him. He must have heard hundreds of stories about her from Aunt Spicy, everyone ending up the same way, "Way you talk, way you act— why Rap, you and your mama like two peas in a pod." He'd seen a picture of her once when she wasn't any older than Cassie Mapp, and he'd tried real hard to cry because he knew she died when he was born. Only thing, the face on the paper looking at him was the same as his.

He remembered his Granny Josie even though Aunt Spicy said he was too little when she died for him to remember anything. He did, though. He remembered the ear aches and the warm oil and Granny talking low and soft as she held her palm close against the side of his head.

"He past and gone," was all Aunt Spicy would ever say about his daddy. He never missed having a daddy because there was always Aunt Spicy or Old Dan Creek, and that was enough.

The "S" was too hard to carve. He settled for a big period as deep as a nail hole after the "I".

"Rap!"

He grabbed up the two jars and headed for the house.

"Where in the Lord's green earth have you been, boy?" Aunt Spicy stood beside the stove, steam from the boiling chicken misting the kitchen window. "Here I sent you down for green beans and plum butter. What did you bring me? Stewed tomatoes and mincemeat. Should have your head examined. How you ever going to grow up to be somebody sitting in that old cave half the day?"

Rap turned and headed back out the door. In a cave it was easier to be somebody.

"All right then, go," Aunt Spicy finally said. "Didn't I hear you thinking about Dan Creek and catfish?"

Aunt Spicy always heard what he was thinking. Sometimes she heard even before he thought.

"And if you just happen to be going that way, take these fresh biscuits to Dan. He's been eating poorly this spring."

Rap hurried across the pasture, not thinking once about climbing the hickory again, crossed over Big Hill, and ran all the way down to the stream.

Dan was not in his usual chair, but when Rap looked in the open door, he saw the old man sprawled out asleep on his cot. He set Spicy's biscuits on the table and pulled his hook and line from under the porch step.

Rap never used a pole nor bobber, just a line wrapped around his finger and a grub on a hook. He sat down on the bank, his bare feet dangling in the water, and watched a leaf, carried by the current, float downstream. Dan had taught him there was a feel to fishing. "Talk to Brother Fish. Tell him about the fat grub you got."

"You live around here?" A voice came from behind him.

Rap spun around. It was the man he had seen from the top of the hickory, only taller and bigger he looked now, leaning up against a tree.

"Yes, sir," Rap answered.

"Seen Dan Creek around?" The man took off his hat and wiped his forehead. When he talked his mouth moved, but nothing else in his face changed. He wasn't frowning, but somehow he looked angry, and his eyes slid right over Rap.

"Dan in his cabin. Taking a nap."

"Taking a nap?" The man stared down at the water and without looking up asked, "Who are you?"

"I be Anson J. Davis," Rap answered, jigging his fishline closer to a willow branch that sagged into the water.

"Davis?" The man straightened up, took a step toward Rap, then stopped. Rap huddled deeper into the weeds. The man looked so fierce Rap was afraid he was going to grab him and shake more words from him.

"Stand up, boy. Let's see what you look like." The voice was low and threatening.

Rap wound his fishline around a twig and stood, his feet squishing down into the mud as he climbed up the bank.

"They call you Anson J., do they?"

"Call me Rap."

"Rap Davis, huh." The man's eyes were black slits under heavy eyebrows. "Your daddy around?"

"Ain't got none. Aunt Spicy say he past and gone."

"Does she?" The man was so tall his shadow spread across the grass and squiggled over the water. "Sounds like her."

"You know my Aunt Spicy?"

"Met her. Not likely to forget her." The man inspected his boots, now mud-splotched, stepped back up the bank, and wiped them clean on the long grass; then he squinted up into the sun, his face a deep copper. "This Aunt Spicy of yours. She thinking about going to Athabasca?"

"Aunt Spicy say we ain't talking the word."

"That's her too. If she don't talk about it, in her mind it stops being." His voice sounded as if he were chewing on a sour plum. "When you get home, you tell her for me that . . . Hey! You got a bite, boy! Tend your line."

Rap scrambled down the bank, grabbed the line, and teased a fat catfish to shore. It lay in the grass, whitish blue belly throbbing, mouth gaping like a toothless, whiskered old man. Rap wriggled the hook loose and held it up by the gills.

"A big one!" he said, looking up, but the stranger was gone.

Rap was still standing on the bank holding the fish when Dan Creek called to him from upstream. "What you doing, boy? Waiting to see if that fish turns into a bird and flies? Kill it or throw it back. Can't live out of water."

"You have him." Rap held out the fish. "You kill it. I can't do that part."

"Everything part of everything else," Dan said taking the fish and picking up a rock. "Sometimes you have to kill to live."

Rap waited until Dan was finished and the fish lay motionless in the grass. "Who that man?"

"What man?"

"Man looking for you. Big. Kind of mean looking."

"Wearing boots? Big hat?"

Rap nodded.

"My son. Been away for a few years. Looks like he's back again, don't it?"

"What's his name, Dan?"

"Creek."

"I know that. His other one."

"Jesse."

It was dusk before Rap and Aunt Spicy finished chores. The barn was full of shadows when he filled his pail with corn for the pigs, and eyes like Jesse Creek's peered down at him from the hayloft, and arms, long and burly, reached out from every corner. Not that he was scared to walk up to the house alone, but he waited by the barn door for Aunt Spicy to finish milking.

Bullfrogs karrumped from Salt Creek and an owl hooted from the top of the plum tree as the shadow of Big Hill crept over the valley. They sat together on the porch steps for their "mullin-time"—"We mull things through so's we can start fresh in the morning," Aunt Spicy always said.

"Was thinking backwards today," she began, snuggling Rap close, "to when your Granny Josie and me and your mama Ann first come to this valley. We walk, you know, all the way from the Louisiana Delta, looking for a place to make a home for your mama, she hardly bigger than a tick."

Rap was glad Aunt Spicy wasn't going to tell

one of her scary stories about knocks at midnight or blackbirds beating on windows or ghosts who carried off boys who told fibs.

"We came up to a cabin here in Creek Country, and we was hot and tired and thirsty, so's I knocked 'specting to see a white face. They'd been taking over Indian land, covering the place like a snowstorm. Well, the door opened and I near died. Here was this big, beautiful, black face looking out at me and I got all flustered at seeing one of ours and I say, 'Please, ma'am, can we get some drinkin' water?' Then she laughed this big laugh that rumbled out into the dark and said, 'What you please-ma'amin' Lulu for?' "

Rap knew the story well. Sometimes he didn't listen to the words, only to the soft ups and downs of Aunt Spicy's voice.

"After while, Lulu's man and her boy show up. Been hunting. Boy, just a little tyke, was all tuckered. Same age as your mama, he was. Lulu's man told us then there was a squatter's cabin beyond the hill a piece that was ours for the taking. We took. Fixed up the shack, cleared the land, built this house here and found a place where we could stay as long as we lived."

"Then we are not going to ... to that ... you know ... to that word we ain't talking."

"What you sayin, boy. Make sense."

"Athabasca."

Aunt Spicy laughed and hugged him closer. "No reason to. Can't be nothing better than we got right here. How come you thinking Athabasca, anyway?"

"That kin of Dan Creek's ..." Rap began. Spicy's arm stiffened.

"What kin?"

"Dan say his name Jesse."

"What you know about him?"

"Saw him when I was fishing. He one mean-look-
ing man."

"Keep clear of him then. He ain't got no business with us. He talk to you?" Spicy's voice was
sharp.

"He ask questions."

"Like what?"

"He ask if we be going to Athabasca."

"None of his concern what we do. Just remember that."

Rap felt as if he were being scolded, and for
once he hadn't done anything bad—at least nothing he could think of.

"That Jesse sure one big man, though. Someday,
maybe, I be that big."

"Someday you might," Spicy answered in a tight
little voice. "Important thing is being big from
neck up. Now you run along to bed. I got my own
mullin' to do."

When Rap went up to his room, he looked under
his bed and poked behind the curtains just to be
sure there wasn't a Jesse Creek hiding in his room.

THREE

"**R**ap, you growing so fast. Busting right out of your britches," Aunt Spicy said as she brushed his good black pants so hard she almost knocked him over. Spicy had his white shirt starched so stiff he crinkled when he moved. "That's what Sundays are for. Getting clean from the outside in and the inside out."

Clearview Pentecostal Baptist Church was a mile's walk with Aunt Spicy in her print dress and wide flowered hat and no chance for Rap to catch the frog that hopped across the road in front of them or to climb the sycamore at the crossroads to see if there were any baby squirrels.

The Mapps were already in their pew, Cassie so clean, all in white, she looked as if she'd squeak if you touched her. The Irby twins were up in front, of course, giggling, and the big Smolletts loitered outside waiting for Nimrod Toles to ring the last bell. Bertha Sneed was already seated in the choir, Bertha with a voice that sounded as if she held a blade of grass between her palms and blew, and she could hold a note longer than anyone else and

33

she always did, which slowed everybody else down so the hymns went on forever.

Just like always, one minute before Reverend Sneed was about to begin his preaching, Mr. and Mrs. James Jackson and Lacey marched up the aisle and settled into the first pew just like they owned it. Aunt Spicy said that was no lie. Jackson did own most everything in Clearview: the newspaper, real estate office, furniture and undertaking parlor, and most of the farmland around.

"Hot. Blazing hot it was. Hotter than the Louisiana Delta in August," Reverend Sneed preached. "Sizzling in sunshine, dry as the desert, and desert it was."

Already the folks were fanning themselves and Rap felt his white shirt dampen with sweat. How did Reverend Sneed do it? One minute he was just a little, tiny man, no taller than Aunt Spicy, and so black he was almost purple, standing there behind the pulpit in his preaching outfit, and the next thing his words rolled out deep and heavy like the voice of God Himself.

"Deep down in Egypt land. Hauling and pushing. Toting and shoving. Sweating and dying. All deep down in Egypt land." Reverend Sneed acted it all out for them so that by the time they were up to the first plague that came to that Pharoah, Rap felt like he'd been tromped on by Old Bones and all three pigs.

Always before, he'd kind of thought Daniel and all them boys in the fiery furnace was his favorite story, but this was better; just one awful plague after another. That Pharoah should have paid more mind. Maybe he needed Moses AND Mrs. Crumpton.

Somewhere between the pyramids and the Red

Sea, Rap got lost. Afterwards he wasn't sure where he'd been. Maybe watching the heavy pendulum of the clock on the front wall, but then he heard the Reverend parting the waters, and the next thing, Mrs. Sneed and the Pentecostal choir were singing up such a storm they could have drowned Pharoah and all his armies by themselves.

After the last amens and just as folks were getting up to leave, the Reverend motioned everyone to sit down again. This time he talked in his real voice. "Brothers and sisters. There's to be an important meeting next Saturday afternoon at the school. Want you all to come. We going to talk on Athabasca." When he spoke the word it sounded as if he were saying "amen" all over again.

"Reverend Sneed, he talking that word," Rap said as they walked home from church. "Can we talk it yet?"

"That's why we having Mrs. Crumpton to dinner. She don't hold no truck with what some folks planning, moving up to that north place."

Having Mrs. Crumpton come for Sunday dinner was like sitting across from a dictionary. Say one word and she'd spend half an hour explaining. Rap decided she got that way from being a teacher.

All Aunt Spicy did was mention Athabasca, and Mrs. Crumpton was off talking about all the wonderful things in Clearview and how anybody would be a fool to leave. She talked right through the stewed chicken and didn't hardly finish until the last bite of sweet potato pie was gone. By that time Aunt Spicy looked as if she'd been caught in the middle of an Oklahoma twister.

The only thing that stopped Mrs. Crumpton was when Spicy looked out the window. "Why, there's

James Jackson and Lacey. Said he'd come by this afternoon. Call them in Rap. I'll just cut another piece of pie here."

Mr. Jackson and Lacey were still dressed up for church, but they didn't look near as uncomfortable as Rap felt.

"Come right in and sit down." Spicy put a slice of pie on the table and picked up Rap's plate. "Rap, why don't you and Lacy run outside and play. Mind you, don't get dirty. And where's Mrs. Jackson?"

"She going to come, but she suffering in the legs today." Mr. Jackson pulled his chair up to the table, unbuttoned his coat, and surveyed the pie as if he were considering buying it. "Now boys," he called. "You heard Miz Davis. Mind what she say. No running off to the creek. Stay right here in Miz Davis door yard and keep out of trouble."

It didn't sound like much fun to Rap, but it was better than staying inside and listening to Mrs. Crumpton and Lacey's father bragging up Clearview all afternoon.

Lacey marched down the steps just as sober as if he were going to church again. Rap raced down after him, but when Lacey got to the bottom step, he stuck out his foot, and Rap had all he could do to keep from tumbling in the dust of the yard.

"Lacey Jackson! I gonna get you some day. You just wait."

"You don't scare me none. What's to do around here? If we was in town at my house we could ride my pony or play with my new marbles."

"We could look for crawdaddies. Or frogs."

"Didn't you hear what my daddy say? We got to stay round here."

"Hey. I know," Rap suggested. "Let's go swing chickens."

"What you talking about? Swing chickens."

"Ain't you never swung chickens? Boy, you dumb, Lacey Jackson."

"Us city folks don't know about swinging no chickens. 'Sides your Aunt Spicy won't want us messing out there."

"Won't care if she don't know. Come on." Rap started around the corner to the hen house. "I'll show you. It's like being one those magicians Mrs. Crumpton talk about. Them guys in circuses that hypnotize people. Remember?"

"What we do?" Lacey peered into the henhouse.

"First you catch one like this. See? Grab her feet with one hand. Get her beak with the other. That's to keep them from squawking. Now tuck her head under her wing and just rock her back and forth like this 'til she goes to sleep. Now, I set her down real careful. See? She ain't moving."

"How long she stay that way?" Lacey stared at the hen, lying motionless at his feet.

"Long time. You try one. Here I help you catch one. We see who get the most chickens to sleep first. We have a contest."

Soon Aunt Spicy's chicken pen was littered with sleeping hens.

"That's four apiece," Lacey shouted. "Last one's mine." He darted into the henhouse.

Rap leaned back against the fence, trying hard not to laugh. The only chicken left was Old Red, who was the "biggest, meanest, peckinest rooster in Okfuskee County" according to Aunt Spicy.

Everything was quiet, but not for long. A minute after Lacey disappeared inside the henhouse door, the noise began. Rap couldn't decide what was loudest: the flapping of Old Red's wings, his angry squawks, or Lacey's yell of pain. By the time Lacey came flying out the door, the rooster's neck outstretched behind him, the hens were beginning to wake up and weave around in circles, and Rap was doubled up, laughing so hard he couldn't stop.

He did stop, though, when Aunt Spicy and Mrs. Crumpton and Mr. Jackson came stomping around the corner of the house. At first they didn't say anything, and Rap knew that was a real bad sign.

Mr. Jackson took charge. He backed both Lacey and Rap up against the side of the henhouse and stood towering over them, his eyes on the sky as if he were talking to God instead of them. "This is the Sabbath! You are to keep it holy." His voice was even bigger than Reverend Sneed's. "Honor thy father and mother or Miz Crumpton or Miz Davis, and stay out of trouble. Now, don't you two go out of this yard. You got one more chance."

He turned and with Aunt Spicy and Mrs. Crumpton marching after him they walked back to the house.

Rap waited until they were gone and then he poked Lacey in the ribs. "Told you I'd get you. You been got good. Anybody'd have more sense than to go messing with a big old mean rooster."

"You and your hypnotizing!" Lacey leaned up against the plum tree and rubbed the scratch on his cheek.

Cassie Mapp's dog had come barking down the road, attracted by the chickens' squawking, and now he lay panting in the shade beside Rap.

"Millard," Rap tousled the dog's head, "you smell

like you been down in Salt Creek rolling in fish.
Got a new batch of fleas too, haven't you?"

"You know what, Rap. You talking about magicians. Bet you never been to a circus."

" 'Course not. No circus never come to Clearview."

"I see one once."

"Where'd you see a circus?"

"When I down in Texas with my daddy bringing
folks up here to Clearview."

"How come you never told me?"

"Saving it. Don't tell everything I know. But this
here circus was a flea circus."

"Don't believe you. You making it up."

"Honest. There was this man in a tent and he
had all these fleas in a little box, and he had them
running races and everybody betting on which one
would jump highest. Hey, Rap. Let's us have a flea
circus. Millard won't miss them."

"What we put them in?"

"Get a matchbox. Maybe you'd better bring a
cover."

In no time they had captured at least twenty
fleas in Aunt Spicy's matchbox.

"Now," Lacey directed, "we got to get them out
on something flat so's we can see them jump. Let's
go up on the porch. In the sun."

The white cushion on one of Spicy's porch chairs
was perfect. "See?" Lacey said. "We can let them
out two at a time. This one's mine. Bet a penny
mine'll jump farther than yours."

Rap put his flea on the edge of the cushion next
to Lacey's. It was hard to pick it up without squash-
ing it, but he managed. The only trouble was neither of the fleas wanted to race. They both just sat

there and began crawling in tiny circles and trying to burrow into the cloth.

"These fleas as dumb as Millard," Rap grumbled. "Don't even know how to jump."

For once Lacey agreed. "Gotta train them. Bet if we put the box on the other side and opened the cover just a crack, why these old fleas go hopping back to their family. Want to try?"

They were just starting the race again when Aunt Spicy opened the porch door. "Right out here. We can sit and take the breeze."

Rap was pretty sure Aunt Spicy wouldn't take too kindly to a flea race on her porch. He grabbed the matchbox, shoved it under the edge of the cushion, and tugged Lacey to his feet. "Come on. We take turns pushing each other in the swing."

"Sit on the steps, boys," Mr. Jackson ordered. "We be going home in a minute."

"Here, Mrs. Crumpton," Aunt Spicy directed. "Take this chair. It more comfortable with the cushion and all."

Rap glanced back over his shoulder to see the matchbox flatten as Mrs. Crumpton sat down.

"Yes, I think we are all agreed," Mrs. Crumpton said, settling into her chair, "that we all must go to the meeting and try to convince Reverend Sneed and the others that we belong here in Clearview and not in some far-off Athabasca."

"Glad that's all settled," Mr. Jackson said. "And you agree, Spicy? You being one of our earliest settlers here in Clearview, your opinion means a lot to folks."

"It takes a lot to change my mind, James. Seems like right here the place to be."

Mrs. Crumpton shifted in her chair and plucked at her skirt.

"You have some uneasy feelings about the matter, Mrs. Crumpton?" Mr. Jackson turned toward her.

"Oh. Oh no. I'm quite comfortable with our decision," she answered, rubbing first one hip then the other.

Rap sneaked a look at Lacey, who did not look back, and then at Mrs. Crumpton. In the sunlight Rap could see the fleas having their own jumping contest.

"Well, son." Mr. Jackson stood up. "Time for us to be going. Would you like us to walk you home, Mrs. Crumpton?"

"Thank you, yes." Mrs. Crumpton stood up and shook out her skirt. "But on the other hand, I think I'll sit a bit longer." She sat down again.

The "sit a bit" lasted until another bite.

"See you tomorrow, Rap," Lacey said, acting as if he'd never heard of a flea circus in his life.

Rap was sure Mrs. Crumpton didn't know anything about flea circuses either, but she sure was in the middle of one, whether she knew it or not. First one flea would hop clean from the floor to the edge of her skirt; then another, Rap was pretty positive it was Lacey's jumped all the way down from Mrs. Crumpton's head and landed somewhere in the vee of her dress.

Pretty soon Mrs. Crumpton had her handkerchief out fanning the air and making little dabs here and there on her neck and elbows and even down at the bottom of her skirt where Rap supposed her ankles were.

"I believe," she said, shaking herself out of the

chair, "I will go along with you, James." She shook
out her skirt again. "You know there's school tomorrow, boys, and I've got an itch to get to your
lessons." She turned, picked up the cushion, pulled
out the matchbox and handed it to Aunt Spicy. "I
see my science lessons have not gone astray, Mrs.
Davis. Both these young men here have become
fine collectors of the *siphonapteia* of wingless
insects."

Aunt Spicy took one look at her matchbox.
"Fleas?" she cried.

Mrs. Crumpton walked sedately down the steps.
"Fleas, indeed. I think Lacy and Anson and I shall
have a long discussion about fleas after school
tomorrow night."

Upstairs in his bedroom, the sun still shining,
Rap decided he hadn't been hungry and didn't
want his supper anyway.

FOUR

The Athabasca meeting, the next Saturday, looked like eighth grade graduation with folks filing up the steps to the schoolhouse, even more people than had been at Bodie Braden's funeral the month before.

"You best stay out here," Aunt Spicy said, hurrying up the steps. "Not going to be room for everyone. Listen through the window."

The last to arrive were Mr. and Mrs. James Jackson and Lacey. The five little Mapps had cabbaged on to all the swings, and the Smollets and the big Toleses had taken over the ball diamond. Cassie Mapp perched on the top step, reading a book. Cassie was always trying to show off how educated she thought she was.

"Wasn't so crowded, I'd go in. Find out more about this Athabasca thing." Rap stuck his hands in his britches' pockets and leaned up against the stair rail. "It's way north. Up where there's Eskimos and fat fish."

"Fat fish!" Cassie snapped her book shut. "Where you learn such trash? No fat fish. You just made that up.

43

"North as far as you can go. I know that for sure."

"It's homestead land. That means ..." Cassie folded her hands on her book, the way Mrs. Crumpton always did when somebody asked a question. "... that means a person can get one hundred sixty acres free for clearing the land."

"How you know all that?"

"I listen."

"Then what's this big meeting for? Suppose you know all about that too?" Rap slid down and sat on the step beside her.

"Of course. Nimrod Toles was over last week and told my daddy all about it. I listened from upstairs. See, Mr. Toles and Reverend Sneed and Isaiah Murphy went up there while back and looked over the place. Everybody in church chipped in money so's they could go."

"I didn't chip no money."

"Bet your Aunt Spicy did."

"Did not."

"Did too. Now them"—she tipped her head toward the schoolhouse—"they deciding if we all going up."

"Everybody?"

"Sure. Everybody. What you think. Whole town's going. Whole county. Maybe the whole state. Us colored, I mean."

"How come folks want to leave here?"

Cassie placed her book carefully on the step, straightened her skirt, cleared her throat just like Mrs. Crumpton.

Giggles and screams mingled with the squeak of the playground swings and the crack of a baseball bat. Rap felt as if he were in school again while everybody else was having recess.

"Because, Rap Davis, in case you haven't noticed there is white folks in this world and there is black folks."

"Red folks too," Rap interrupted.

"Of course, but they don't matter right now. Simple fact is, those white folks is just plain, downright ignorant because they don't want us to have our own place here in Clearview or be able to vote. You know what vote means, don't you?"

"Sure do. It's what Nimrod Toles didn't get."

"And no other colored man will either, 'less we have a county all our own. And," she said, her voice getting shriller, "that's why we're going to Athabasca, where there ain't no grandfather clause nor Jim Crow."

"What's grandfathers got to do with voting?"

" 'Cause, unless all of our grandfathers were white or could read or something like that, we can't do nothing except what white folks tell us."

Cassie didn't know what she was talking about, that was for sure. No white folks had ever told Rap what to do. In fact, he hardly ever saw one. There weren't any living in Clearview nor Boley nor even in Weleetka, and even if there had been, he was pretty sure they wouldn't bother him none. Only white man he'd seen up real close was Sam Kelly, who came through town once a month or so selling stuff from his wagon.

Reverend Sneed's voice came booming through the window. "Stay here and Old Jim Crow'll peck your eyes out. Peck your tongue out. Peck your heart out. First thing you know going to be a new law. Why, we go over to Muskogee, and they won't

let us in their stores even if we have the money to
buy. Won't let us on their trains 'less we sit in front
where soot and ashes come raining down on us.
They have their way, we be walking in the streets
while they use the sidewalks. That's Jim Crow,
and he's coming right here to Okfuskee County,
Oklahoma, before you know it."

"Amen! Amen!" came a chorus of agreement.

Then Mrs. Crumpton's voice soared over the rest,
just like a regular schoolday, and just like regular
schoolchildren the grown-up folks got real quiet
and even Rap listened hard.

"Reverend Sneed. Why leave the rich land here,
as fine a land as lays out of doors? Why leave our
sunshine, our fine school for a land of ice and
cold? Of course there are problems here, but there
are problems everywhere on earth and even in the
waters beneath the earth. Opportunity is all around.
It is here within hand's grasp. Now you talk of
transporting folks clear up to this Athabasca to be
costing five thousand dollars you say. Why five
thousand dollars would operate a fine business
right here in Clearview that would be a credit to
us. Let us cease to ramble here and there and be
content in our beloved Clearview. I say to you, I
plead with you. Let down your buckets where you
are."

The amens rang out again, but Rap wasn't sure
whether everyone was agreeing or whether Mrs.
Crumpton was just one powerful talker.

It got real quiet then until Rap heard Nimrod
Toles. It wasn't hard to tell who was talking.
Nimrod had a voice like an untuned banjo string—
twangy and flat. "We stay here long enough . . . it

won't be buckets being let down . . . It be colored bodies from lynching trees."

Then Mr. Jackson and Mr. Edwards and Mr. Murphy and Mr. Adcock and Mr. Evans and Mr. Johnson all talked one after the other—some of them for and some of them against—and then everybody was talking all at the same time and as hard as he listened, Rap couldn't make sense out of a word.

"Let's go play on the teeter-totter." Seemed like even Cassie was getting tired of listening to all the words swirling around inside.

"Naw!" Rap shook his head. "You always try to bounce me off. You know you do. And I ain't gonna be bounced no more. I'm getting too big for that."

"Won't bounce you. Promise. Cross my heart. We just teeter real nice and easy. And you can choose which end you want."

Rap chose the end that faced the schoolhouse. When he was up in the air, he could see right through the windows into the meeting, and best of all there weren't any splinters on his end of the board. He had to find just the right place to sit to balance Cassie. Even if he was taller, she was heavier.

Cassie kept her promise. He felt just like that old crow, soaring up and floating down and then up again.

"See. I can do it with no hands." Cassie folded her arms across her chest and she loomed above him at the far end of the teeter.

"Me too. Real easy."

Up and down they went, faster and faster. Just when Rap was busy thinking about how he might even be able to see all the way up to Athabasca if he teetered high enough, Cassie did it.

He was clear up at the top balancing with no hands when Cassie straightened her knees and slammed her end of the board into the dirt so hard that he bounced to one side and then to the other and flew off, landing on the ground on the seat of his best britches.

"Rap Davis! What you doing there in the dirt with your best duds on?" Aunt Spicy marched down the schoolhouse steps.

"Why Miz Davis," Cassie said as if her mouth were full of honey, "Rap here was pretending he could fly. Showing off with no hands and he just flang himself off."

"Well, he can just flang himself up and come along home with me."

As he followed Aunt Spicy out of the schoolyard, he turned around, stuck out his tongue so far it hurt, and vowed he'd get that old Cassie Mapp one day and he'd get her real good.

By the time he caught up with Aunt Spicy, she was three fenceposts down the road toward home, setting her feet so hard that she left heel marks in the dirt.

"What we going to do about Athabasca, Aunt Spicy? We all going to pack up and go or we going to stay here with our buckets?" That showed he could listen just as good as Cassie Mapp.

Aunt Spicy looked down at him and brushed the red dust off the sleeve of his shirt. "Tell you true, my mind's unsettled. Now Reverend Sneed, he makes a right good argument. All the land a body could want, good land, cheap land. Course, it ain't red like this. He told how him and the rest come near to walking their boots off, way up north there, looking for dirt this color. Wasn't none."

"What color they find?"

"Gray, Nimrod say."

"Gray!" Rap stopped still in the middle of the road. Red dirt, red folks. Black dirt, black folks. Gray dirt . . . maybe that snow and ice not cold enough to suck their color all the way out.

Spicy stopped and waited for him. "Worst thing about it," she went on. "Won't be no school."

"No school!" Rap forgot about gray folks. A place to live with no school. Why that put him right in mind of Reverend Sneed's sermon about the Garden of Eden. Then and there Rap knew Athabasca was the place for him. All he'd have to do was make Aunt Spicy see things the right way.

"When we going to know, Aunt Spicy? When we going to know what we decide?"

"We stay here! Take a mighty strong sign to change my mind." She started walking again.

He should have guessed. Of course there'd be no school. It was plain enough that Mrs. Crumpton didn't have no intention of going to Athabasca and Mrs. Crumpton WAS school. He was doing his best to keep from laughing right out loud when he spied the man coming toward him.

Even though the sun was warm and it was broad daylight and Aunt Spicy was right beside him and he was ten years old, he felt little cold prickles all the way down his backbone. Rap knew it was that Jesse Creek even if he couldn't quite make out the man's face. It was something about the way he walked, so determined, like he could smash through a barn wall and not even notice it was there.

"Come on, boy." Spicy's voice came so sudden it

nearly made him jump. "Let's us just cut across
the field down to the creek and home. Want to see
if the fiddlehead fern is up yet. Fancy me a salad."
She didn't wait for his answer.

As they walked the plowed ground, Rap wondered if she'd recognized Jesse Creek, but there
was something about the stiffness of her back that
made him decide not to ask. Even Rap knew there
wouldn't be no fiddlehead fern for at least another
month.

That night after supper when Rap had wiped
and put away the last plate in the cupboard, he
and Spicy sat out on the porch.

"Do you suppose my Granny Josie would?"

"Suppose your Grannie Josie *would* anything,
but what you talking about?" Spicy unlaced her
heavy work shoes and set them side by side on the
step.

"Athabasca."

"Your granny might go. She'd get tired of one
place and leave. Always ready to jump up and
move on. Why there we was, down on the delta,
nothing left of our family after the War except
your granny and me—your own mother no more
than half your age. Your granny heard about
Clearview. She'd heard Oklahoma was going to be
a colored state and we could all be free and black
together."

"Bet there weren't no schools here then, either."

"Wasn't nothing. Hard at first, but we had a
right nice place here. Then, about ten years or so
before you was born, they had this big white land
rush, so's even Nimrod Toles couldn't get elected
as county supervisor nor any other colored man
either. Now it's getting to be so's there's more of

them than there is of us, so's they in the driver's seat."

Rap lowered his head to hide the grin spreading across his face so far his ears moved. If Spicy kept going, she'd talk herself right into Athabasca without any signs or nothing.

"Not easy to be American and colored." She leaned her elbow on one knee, cradling her chin in her palm. " 'Course who's to say it'd be any better in a few years up north. Us colored seem to be some kind of problem to everybody 'cept ourselves."

"Ain't no white folks 'round here."

"Got nothing against them one by one, but you put them together in a bunch, and you got something else. They just naturally stick together and try to take over most everything. Give them an inch, they take a mile. Move in where they're not wanted, act all uppity, and push their ways. Sometimes it looks like the only thing for us to do is pack up and move on to some better place."

"This Athabasca a better place?" Rap urged.

"Then there's the other hand . . ."

Aunt Spicy's other hand worried Rap more than her first hand.

"Mrs. Crumpton look this Athabasca place up in her geography book," Spicy went on, "and she say winter last most year round and the sun only manages to get up there three months out of whole year. Don't hardly see how a crop'd grow. Take a right strong sign to tell me to move away from Clearview."

When Rap went to bed that night, he fell asleep thinking up right signs that Spicy might believe.

FIVE

The next Saturday morning, when Spicy sent him to the store, signs were posted all over town: big signs, little signs, some printed by the *Clearview Patriarch*, some little and handwritten, stuck in the corner of store windows—CLEARVIEW HOME-SEEKERS EXCURSION, May 9-11, 1910.

Rap walked into town, making like he was as important as James Jackson and all of Clearview was his. He leaned against the corner of the depot and watched the shiny rails sliding past, all the way east to Fort Smith and all the way west for over a hundred and twenty-four miles. New rails, they were, no more than four or five years old, Spicy said, rails that could take him almost anywhere.

When he got to be somebody, he'd ride those rails in a fancy car with plush drapes over the windows, and he'd have his name *A. J. Davis* in gold and black painted on the outside. "Who this A. J. Davis?" people'd ask, and he'd be sitting back in his soft and velvety seat, not even bothering to look out the train window at all the people staring at him.

A train would be coming in soon. Lacey Jackson showed him a penny once that he'd put on the track and let a train run over, and it was all squished out, flat as paper with old Abe Lincoln's face splattered out smooth. Rap traded Lacey his own good penny for the flat one, but when he took it into Mrs. Doggett's grocery store to buy a stick of red licorice, she wouldn't take it. Lacey laughed and laughed and went off jingling his pocket full of pennies to show off how important he was.

The sun had cleared High Hill to the east, and the scrub oak glistened, outlining the steep hump. He sat down on the depot platform and dangled his legs over the rails.

"Hey, Rap. How'd you like to make some money?" Lacey Jackson came around the corner, his arms loaded with signs, tacked onto pointed sticks.

"Doing what?"

"Putting up these signs."

Rap read the words: "Lots for Sale—$10 down, balance by month. See James E. Jackson, President of Clearview Land Agency."

"Nothing to it." Lacey threw the signs down in front of Rap. "You take them over behind the schoolhouse. You start at Mrs. Adcock's and walk fifty steps and stick one in the ground. Fifty steps more and stick in another one, until you've used them all up."

"You mean out in Warren's pasture?"

"Yep."

"How much you give me?"

Lacey screwed up his face as if he were figuring numbers in his head. "Give you a nickel. Won't take more than half an hour or so."

"That nickel been under a train? Ain't taking no

flat nickel. And how come your daddy want these signs sticking up in a pasture? Abe Warren not like it."

"Nothing wrong with this nickel. See?" Lacey moved his hand in and out of his pocket so fast that all Rap could see was a flash of silver. "Ain't Warren's pasture anyway. He just lease it from my daddy and with all the folks coming for the Excursion, Daddy he going to sell it for building lots. Now, when you get through with those signs, I meet you at the newspaper, and I pay you the money."

Maybe just this once Lacey was telling the truth. Rap gathered up the signs. Besides he could use the nickel. He hadn't tasted candy for so long, he'd about forgot what his favorite flavor was.

Straight down Main Street he walked, the signs over his shoulder like a general holding a whole bunch of flags or guns or something, past Mr. Doggett's Staples, Fancy Groceries and Dry Goods Store, past the Clearview Drug, across the street to Mrs. Atkins Hotel. He stopped and looked in the window of Carpenter's Confections, Candies, and Cider Store with its licorice, gum drops, corn candy, and a big fat chocolate bar all wrapped up in red and blue with a picture of what was inside if you were to take a knife and slice through the rich sweetness. He'd spend his nickel for that bar. It even had nuts stuck in the caramel underneath the chocolate coat.

Adcock's hound dog greeted him with a grunt and curled up in the chair on the front porch, head on his paws, watching him with half-closed eyes.

Rap put his foot down at Warren's fence and began to count as he walked, "One, two, three, four . . ." Fifty steps was a long piece. "Fourteen, fifteen, sixteen." He detoured around a water hole and wondered if he should count those steps too. At fifty he pushed the sign into the dirt, glad the ground was soft from last night's rain.

"One, two, three, four . . ." A toad jumped out from a clump of grass. He set the signs down and dropped to his knees. "You all shrunk up and skinny, Mr. Toad. Been living in that dark hole all winter, I bet. All hungry and thirsty, aren't you? Eyes like big gold buttons, you got."

Cassie Mapp and Lacey Jackson yelled and made a fuss anytime they saw a toad. They said if you touched one you got warts, big bumpy warts all over your hands and face and neck. Of course, you could always get rid of the warts with milkweed juice, except milkweeds weren't big enough to have juice yet. Rap, he liked toads. They were one of his favorite things because they didn't do nothing and they weren't good for nothing. He never heard of anyone eating a toad. Frog legs, but no toad legs. A toad was a safe thing to be. He almost had him, but the toad jumped clean through Abe Warren's fence.

He went back, picked up his signs. Now where was he? Was it fourteen steps when he saw the toad? No. Nearer thirty or thirty-five. "Thirty-six, thirty-seven, thirty-eight."

Only two signs in. It was going to take him all morning. Half-hour, Lacey had said. Rap stopped dead in his tracks and looked around. It was just plumb silly. All the signs said the same thing about the same place. There wasn't no sense in stringing them out clear across the pasture. It'd look a lot more important if all the signs were stuck together in one spot. Somebody'd notice them then, sticking up there, one after the other, like teeth in a comb.

Ahead the pasture sloped down to a tiny ravine. The ground was soft, and it didn't take any time at all to plunk the rest of the signs in a neat row, each one almost touching the next. He looked back toward Adcock's. People could see them, that was for sure, and that was the purpose—to get all those new folks from down south to come up here to Clearview and make the town the biggest city in Oklahoma. That's what Lacey's daddy kept saying at all the town meetings.

Lacey Jackson was waiting for him just outside the newspaper office. "Told you it wouldn't take more'n a half hour or so."

Lacey always timed everything: how long recess was, how long it took to walk to school. Once he even timed how long Mrs. Crumpton could go on talking without stopping. All that just because of the pocketwatch he got last Christmas. Any excuse at all, and Lacey would haul that old watch out of his pocket and make like he was somebody really important who had to keep track of the whole world.

"Where's my nickel?" Rap could already taste the creamy chocolate.

"Got to get it from my daddy."

"Thought you had it in your pocket."

"Ought to pay better attention. This's all I got in my pocket." Lacey held out a tinfoil wrapper from a stick of gum. "You want this instead of a nickel? You can have it."

Rap wanted to punch him right in his grinning

face, but he wanted the chocolate bar more. "Reckon I take the nickel."

Lacey didn't have to go inside for his father. Mr. Jackson pushed open his office door. "Well, son. Did you get those signs up?"

"Yes, sir."

"Good boy. Here you are." He counted out five shiny nickels into Lacey's outstretched palm and strode off down the street.

"Which one do you want?" Lacey turned over each coin so that Rap could make his choice.

"How come you get four and I get one and you didn't do nothing?"

" 'Cause I'm the hirer. You be the hiree."

Lacey Jackson! Always making up his own rules, not playing fair in I Spy, always going out and finding another hiding place when he'd already been caught. Cheating, too. Peeking at Rap's spelling and always telling Mrs. Crumpton it was Rap making loud noises in the middle of the pledge of allegiance when it was Lacey doing it himself. And that Cassie Mapp thinking that Lacey some sort of big stuff, she giggling and carrying on brainless like whenever Lacey was around.

Rap started home and didn't even glance at the creamy chocolate bar all wrapped up in its shiny red and blue wrapper there in Carpenter's window. He wasn't hungry for candy any more. Spicy was sweeping the porch when he got there.

"Close your eyes and hold out your hand." He dropped the coin in her palm.

"Where'd you get that nickel? Don't tell me you found it. Round here nickels is too important to be dropping."

"Didn't find it. Earned it. Did a job for Mr. Jackson, putting up signs in Warren's pasture."

"Good morning's wages. We just keep it for something special. Now where's that box of pepper I sent you for?"

"Pepper?"

"Anson J. Davis. Don't tell me you forgot again!"

He was back in town and just tucking the box of pepper in his pocket when he heard the whistle of the noon freight. At night, when he was in bed, and the sound came curling in the window, he thought it was the lonesomest sound he'd ever heard, but in the daylight of a sunny Saturday, the whistle sounded as if it were inviting him to come right down to the station and watch what was going on.

He was all settled on the platform bench when the train came sliding in, black and shiny with gold numbers blazing, puffing out smoke and steam, sparks flying out and the noise and clang and screech so loud he felt his head would burst. With one big whoosh, the train stopped, and soon the whole platform was full of people coming and going, toting boxes and barrels and hurrying past with handcarts taking stuff off and loading stuff on.

He felt the man beside him before he heard his voice.

"Anson J, don't you have nothing better to do than sit here and watch trains?"

It was Jesse Creek towering above him, his thumbs hooked in his belt loops, not looking at Rap, but watching the engine breathing out steam.

Rap sidled down the bench. "I like trains, Jesse Creek."

"Wouldn't like them if you'd worked on them as

long as I have." The man did look at him then, almost smiling. "How'd you know my name?"

"Dan told me."

"What else he tell you?"

"Talk about a lot of things." Rap stared down at the man's boots, leather boots they were, fancy, high-heeled cowboy boots with curlicues of leaves and things running up both sides.

"Like my boots?" The man stretched out his foot and hiked up his pant leg.

"Kinda."

"Stick around. Grow up a bit. Come out to the oil rigs. You can have some too. Out there, don't matter what color you are."

It was a dumb thing to say. As far as Rap could see there wasn't more than a shade of difference between the man's hand that rested up against the depot wall and his own—a little redder, maybe, but that was all.

"Don't want to work in no oil fields. Going to be a judge . . . or a supervisor . . . or a somebody."

This time the man did laugh, right out loud, sort of rusty as if he wasn't used to doing it.

"And all that's going to happen right here in Clearview?"

"Don't want to stay here. Want to go to Athabasca. Aunt Spicy say we go when she gets a sign."

"Athabasca! You know where that is?"

"Sure. Up with Eskimos and fat fish."

"Eskimos and fat fish. Up where there's three months of sun and nine months of ice."

"Land's free. One hundred sixty acres. All we has to do is live on it."

"Or die on it." Jesse Creek jammed his hand in

his pockets, spun around, and walked off past the corner of the depot.

When Rap got home, he set the box of pepper on the kitchen table. Aunt Spicy was shoving wood into the kitchen stove.

"Aunt Spicy, do people die in Athabasca?"

"Suppose. People die everywhere. Why you asking?"

"I was thinking. 'Cause if you can die anywhere, you can be somebody anywhere, can't you?"

"True. Ain't *where* that makes a somebody. It's *who*."

"Don't want to work on no oil rig. Wouldn't want to be that who."

Spicy looked up and frowned. "Why you thinking about oil rigs? Place for drifters. Where you get this oil rig talk?"

"That big Jesse Creek. He told me I get a pair of boots like his if I work out there."

"Better shoes to fill than his. Where you see him?"

"Down when the train come in. He always hanging around."

"That's 'cause he ain't got those boots on the ground yet. He never did stay put. Cowboy, soldier, railroad man. He part Creek, part colored, part nobody. Got nothing against Creek . . . nor colored. Just against nobody. He not half the man his daddy is—Old Dan."

"Old Dan nice."

"He got his ways. We got ours. His tribe treated our people better than some others I could mention."

Spicy was doing it again. Just when he got all the little bits of what he knew and what he'd heard together in one chunk, she'd say something and bust it into a whole bunch of pieces again.

SIX

Mrs. Crumpton closed school for Clearview Home-Seeker Excursion Days. Rap couldn't figure out how to see everything that was going to happen: the Boley ten-piece cornet band, the school program of speeches and plays and singing arranged by Mrs. Crumpton, a baseball game between the Toleses and Smollets and all their relatives, a lecture by Lacey's daddy on "Boost Our Town, Don't Knock it," a public debate by the literary circle of the Daughters of Ethopia on "Morality Increases with Civilization." Rap didn't know what the big words meant, but they sounded important. Best of all, there was to be a big picnic in Warren's pasture.

"Want to make a pile of money, Rap?" Lacey Jackson ran down the school steps. "You too, Cassie."

"Naw." Cassie jumped the last two steps. "Don't need no money. My folks be going to Athabasca. Everything free up there."

"Nothing free nowhere." Lacey stood on the bottom step, staring at the ground.

Cassie tugged at his arm. "We going to own more land up there even than your daddy has."

"Don't care. You not gone yet. You want to make some money or don't you?"

"Not putting up no more signs." Rap turned toward home. "Not buying no more pennies either."

"This be easy. You and Cassie sit down at the railroad station. Me, I meet all these people getting off the train and I make them buy a subscription to my daddy's newspaper. I bring them over to you ... you be sitting at a table, you write down their names and, Cassie, you take the money."

Rap turned around. "How much we get?"

"Daddy say he give us three cents for every subscription."

"Three cents?" Rap looked right into Lacy's eyes.

"Well ... Daddy say five cents, but if there be three, it's easier to divide."

"Who get them extra pennies?"

Lacey shoved his hands into his pockets and looked off toward High Hill as if he were so interested in something up there he couldn't be interrupted.

"We do it for five cents," Cassie said in her Mrs. Crumpton voice. "Then we divide by three."

"All right," Lacey agreed, "but if it don't come out even, I keep that extra for overhead."

"Overhead!" Rap tried to look him in the eyes again, but Lacey was still gazing up at High Hill. "Who this overhead?"

"Don't mind no overhead," Cassie broke in. "We get anything extra, we put it in collection plate come Sunday. That's the place for overheads."

"We going to miss all the fun sitting down there at that old depot selling your daddy's newspapers."

"Won't take all day. We just sell when all these new people that's moving into town come off the train. We be through by noon. Honest. Want to or not?"

"We do it," Cassie said, "and I divide the money."

The next morning Rap settled himself on the depot bench, an upturned crate for a table, with Cassie beside him holding an empty cigarbox for the money.

The excursion train came shooshing to a stop, and the Boley cornet band blared out a welcome. The depot platform, empty only minutes earlier, swirled with town folks greeting relatives and friends who piled from the train laden with baggage and boxes and crates, their voices so loud and shrill they almost drowned out the band.

"I think all Texas come up on that train, Rap," Cassie said, her head swiveling as strange faces went past. "We luckier than some, though."

"What some?"

"Thinking about white folks."

"What you saying? No whites here. What you know about white folks anyway?"

"I been up to Muskogee. Seen lot of them. You know what? They all one color. Us, we come in all colors."

Cassie was right. Rap had never thought about it before. Seeing all the faces getting off the train was like looking up at High Hill when leaves were changing to pretty colors, bright and shining in the sun.

Lacey threaded his way through the crowd, hollering at people and grabbing them by the sleeves and tugging them up to Cassie.

Rap never printed words so fast in his life, and

Cassie's fingers flew, sorting out coins, and making change and doing all the figurings right in her head without ever having to write the numbers down.

By the time the station was empty again, they'd signed up twenty-two new subscribers for the *Clearview Patriarch* and five or six others had promised to stop back later after they'd looked over the lots for sale.

"Twenty-two times five is . . ." Cassie screwed up her face and looked up as if the answer were written in the sky somewhere. "Is . . . is . . . one dollar and ten cents and divided by three is . . . is . . . thirty-six and two-thirds."

Rap thought of Aunt Spicy's pie. "Three-thirds make a penny."

"Sure does." Cassie giggled. "You going to pass arithmetic after all, Rap. Means we each get thirty-six cents and I put two pennies in the collection plate Sunday."

"Told you we'd be through be noon." Lacey leaned over the table and pulled out his watch, holding it out for both to see. "Even got five minutes to spare. Bet we could make a whole pile of money if we started our own business."

"We not old enough. Got to grow up for that and by the time we be growed up, Cassie and maybe me be long gone to Athabasca."

The grin faded from Lacey's face as he tucked his watch into his pocket. Rap wished he could pull his words right out of the air and tuck them back into his mouth.

A shadow fell onto the gleaming coins, and Rap felt someone looking over his shoulder.

"Still selling or have you closed up the office?"

It was Jesse Creek, standing so tall Rap had to bend his head back to see the man's face.

"Yes, sir." Lacey straightened up. *"Clearview Patriarch* fastest growing paper in Okfuskee County. Yours for one whole year just seventy-five cents if you buy today."

"Sounds like I ought to sign up." The man's voice was soft and rumbly.

"How you going to get a paper in them oil fields?" The man was standing too close to Rap.

"Remembered that, did you?" Jesse Creek rested one booted foot up on the bench beside Rap. "Well, I tell you, boy. Don't intend to be there forever. Sooner or later a man needs a place of his own. Where do I sign up for your paper?" He pulled a crisp one-dollar bill from a leather wallet and placed it on the table in front of Rap.

Rap printed the name carefully. "You have a middle name?"

"No. Just Jesse Creek. Isn't that enough?"

Jesse Creek was worse than Mrs. Crumpton, asking questions that didn't have answers.

"Got to do my figgering all over again," Cassie complained as Jessie Creek strode down the length of the platform toward Main Street. "But did you see his money? Must be rich place, them oil fields."

"Aunt Spicy say it's a drifter place."

"That man be drifting this way," Lacey added. "He talk to my daddy last night about buying a place here."

"Something about him," Cassie went on. "He scary."

"Don't scare me none, if he got money," Lacey said gathering up Cassie's coins and putting them in the cigarbox.

"Don't care," Cassie insisted. "He got one kind of hungry look about him, and he was looking at us like we be dinner."

At the picnic in Warren's pasture that noon there was Jesse Creek again, eating his dinner, squatting under a big tree, not looking at anyone, as if he were all alone among the hundreds of folks milling around. Just over the fence, parked along the side of the road, was the biggest, blackest, shiniest car Rap had ever seen: wheels of spoked yellow, steering wheel big as a barrel top polished to a black sheen, dashboard full of watch faces all of them bigger than Lacey's watch, gear shift with a ball on top of polished wood, seats—leather—smelling of cattle ranches and a top now folded and tucked away at the back.

"Oh, look, Cassie!" Rap stood on the running board and ran his hand across the leather seat. "That be somebody. That be somebody who owns this."

"Just a old car. Come on. We get in line for the picnic."

Rap jumped down from the running board and ran around to the front. "Cassie! They like eyes looking at you with this big mouth between." He touched the silver lady balanced on one toe atop the radiator cap and knelt and traced the emblem on the shiny chrome: red, white, and blue, it was, shaped like a shield with *LIBERTY* lettered in gold.

"She's a Liberty eight-cylinder, boy."

Jesse Creek stood over him, his hands locked into his pants pocket, one leg propped up against the glossy bumper.

"Belong to you?" Rap looked up into the thin, smoky eyes.

"Not yet. Thinking about buying it, though. Might come in right handy for getting down to the oil fields from here."

"From here? You figuring on settling here?"

"Figuring maybe."

The man took his hands out of his pockets, brushed the chrome bumper free of dust where his boot had been, and looked up the road.

"Want to go for a spin up High Hill? It'll climb it in second gear without even a sputter."

"Honest? You mean . . . ?"

The man nodded and half smiled.

Aunt Spicy had warned him to keep clear of Jesse Creek, but a ride in a car like this was too good to miss.

"Can Cassie and Lacey come? They my friends."

"Sure. Shinny over the fence and get them. I'll show you how it feels to *really* be somebody."

With Cassie bouncing up and down in the back seat, Lacey beside her, one hand on the leather arm rest as if he were mayor of Clearview, and Rap in the front seat beside Dan Creek's big kin, they took off up the road with a roar, leaving more dust behind than four Smollets could make sliding into home base all at once.

"What do you think?" the big man said, guiding the car with just one hand on the steering wheel.

Rap looked out at the blur of fence posts and bushes and trees flying by. "I think we moving fast!" he gasped.

"We are, boy. Thirty-five miles an hour."

"Like we could just take off and fly if we went any faster."

"I going to be sick!" Lacey cried from the back seat.

Jesse pumped both legs down on the floor pedals and the car lunged to a stop, almost throwing Lacey into the front seat. Jesse ran around and opened the back door.

"I all right now," Lacey said in a thin, tight voice.

Jesse laughed, a big, throaty laugh. "I'll take it a little slower. You get to feeling that way again, put your head between your knees. You'll get used to it."

Up High Hill they zoomed and down again, Cassie still bouncing on the leather seats that swooshed out air every time she landed, and Lacey, head tucked between his knees for the rest of the ride.

With a final surge of power, the big car careened down the narrow lane that bordered Warren's pasture and coasted to a silent stop.

Aunt Spicy stood by the fence, straightening her flowered hat. She didn't look at Rap or Lacey or Cassie. She looked right past Jesse Creek too, but she was talking to him all the same. "So you back, Jesse Creek," she said, her words flat and tired.

"We not gone that long, Aunt Spicy," Rap said climbing out of the front seat. "Just up High Hill and back."

"Don't think that's what she means, boy. Here. You kids take this and get yourselves some lemonade or something." He held out some coins. "Mr. Jackson there needs something in his stomach."

Without looking back, the man shifted the car into gear. "We got some talking to do, Spicy. You and me!"

Spicy didn't answer. The car moved off, leaving her holding onto the fence so tight Rap thought she must be afraid a wind would come and blow her away.

SEVEN

Two nights later, dishes done, Aunt Spicy announced, "No more mullin'. Get dressed. We going to call on Mr. Jackson."

"Mrs. Crumpton be there too?" Rap asked already thinking of reasons to stay home.

"No. Our business be with Lacey's daddy."

"We going to buy a lot from Mr. Jackson?"

"That was what we be talking about, buying and selling."

Jackson's house was the biggest in Clearview, red brick with windows enough for a schoolhouse, fancy front door with panels of glass, and a gravel walk that wound around the side.

"Maybe we have a house like this someday."

Spicy squeezed him tight against her side. "Honey, a good house has a front porch, a back door, and enough love to hold up the roof and we already got that."

Mr. Jackson was home. Mrs. Jackson and Lacey were gone.

"They getting ready for the Sisters of Ethopia meeting," Mr. Jackson explained as he ushered them into a front parlor that smelled as if nobody lived there. It didn't smell bad, just empty. Spicy and Rap sat down on a mohair couch so big Rap's feet barely touched the carpeted floor.

"Now what can I do for you, Spicy?" Mr. Jackson said, leaning back in his chair and looking out over the top of his glasses. "Want to add some more to that twenty-acres of yours? Got some real nice property coming up for sale right to the east of you there."

"Not thinking of buying, James. Thinking of selling."

"Selling!" Mr. Jackson repeated.

If Aunt Spicy was selling, it meant just one thing.

"Athabasca?" Mr. Jackson spat out the word.

"Considering, James. Not for me. For Rap here. He got to have a chance to be somebody."

"Of course he does, Spicy." Mr. Jackson smoothed his pant legs with both palms. "I want the same for Lacey. For all of us. But what's happened? Thought you were dead set against Reverend Sneed's crazy scheme."

"Thought I was too, James, but I never made a promise either way," Spicy said, her mouth tight.

"But we've put down roots here, Spicy. That's what Clearview was meant to be—a place where our people could be together, run our own lives, build our own city, have our own county. Long as we all stick together, we can have a city here that some day will number in the thousands. Why, I've got two men coming in next week who're thinking of opening up a coal mine here. We're going to grow in Clearview."

"What makes you think white folks going to let us do it?" There was a hard edge in Aunt Spicy's voice that Rap had never heard before. "Why, not a week goes by but you don't print a story in that newspaper of yours about a lynching. When I was a slave on the Delta, I didn't read about them. I saw them! Saw Rap's own granddaddy—" Spicy stopped.

"But that isn't now. Not here." Mr. Jackson took off his glasses and rubbed the bridge of his nose.

"Not here yet, James. Bound to come."

"You forget we're free, Spicy. You forget we not slaves anymore. Those days are past. We have our rights."

"Black rights! White wrongs! They get this grandfather clause in, we all might as well be wearing chains and working the road gang."

"I'm not saying it won't take patience, Spicy. And time."

"James Jackson!" Aunt Spicy sat up, planting her feet firmly as if she were going to stand up. "I ain't got time. I ain't got patience to see one of our folks swinging from a white rope again. So don't talk to me about time and patience."

"We can't be bitter, Spicy. We got to think about the race. We mustn't forget that."

"Forget!" Spicy looked as if she were going to pounce on Mr. Jackson. "Not likely I forget what it felt to be a slave. What it felt to be owned by a white man. If your own daddy hadn't escaped, you'd been a field hand back on the Delta with the rest of us, picking cotton and saying, 'Yes, suh.' "

"That's past, Spicy. It's over and done."

"Ain't ever over and done long as us folks has memories."

"You must look to the future, Spicy. Someday, all of us—back, white, red—will be walking down the same road together."

"It ain't walking-together-time yet, James Jackson.

It was like being with an Aunt Spicy he'd never known, not just the way she looked all coiled up on the edge of the sofa like a rattler, but her words came out sharp and crackling like lightning from a thunderstorm.

Mr. Jackson didn't say anything for a while; then he stood up and walked over to the big window that looked out over Clearview's main street. He could have been as old as Aunt Spicy with his mouth all puckered up as if he were going to whistle or maybe even cry.

"Is it all impossible, Spicy? Clearview?"

Spicy pushed herself up from the couch, walked over to Mr. Jackson, and put her hand on his sleeve. "Not impossible, James. Don't make no difference where we dream, just so's we do. Rap here and me think we'll carry our dream to Athabasca along with Reverend Sneed and the Toleses and the rest. That's why I want to sell. And maybe when Rap and your Lacey grow up, freedom won't be a dream no more. It'll be real."

Mr. Jackson turned from the window. "Sounds as if you've already made up your mind. I expect you want me to buy you out?"

"Don't expect no figures tonight. Let me know when you can."

He walked with them to the door. "My boy going to miss you, Rap. He tells me you're his best friend." He stood in the doorway until Rap and Spicy reached the end of the walk.

"When we make up our minds on this Athabasca business, Aunt Spicy?"

Spicy didn't answer. Instead she took his hand

in hers, and they walked along in silence until
they were almost to the crossroads.

"Did you get a sign, like you say?"

"Sometimes signs don't look like nothing. Nothing's what I been seeing lately."

Athabasca! They were going to Athabasca! He
could hardly wait to tell Cassie Mapp and old
Lacey. He and Spicy'd get a farm bigger than all
of Clearview, and they'd build a house bigger than
Lacey's by ten, fifteen, maybe even twenty times
over.

"I know what you thinking, Rap Davis. You thinking of getting right up there on top of High Hill
and shouting our news to all of Clearview. Ain't
you just? Don' you do it! We wait a few days."

"Miz Davis! Miz Davis!" A piercing cry cut
through the dusk and Cassie Mapp, hair ribbons
fluttering in the breeze came running toward them,
her sister Cody two steps behind. "You gotta go!
Man say!"

"Go where? What man you talk about?"

"Car man say so," Cody said, grinning up at
Rap.

"He no car man. 'Sides he didn't have no car."
Cassie pushed Cody aside. "Miz Davis. This man
say you got go. He in one big hurry too."

Aunt Spicy grabbed Cassie by the shoulders.
"Catch your breath, girl. And straighten out your
tongue. First, what man?"

"That Jesse Creek man. The one at the picnic."

"One who drive the big car." Cody tugged at
Spicy's skirt.

"And just where does Jesse Creek expect me to
go?"

"Why Miz Davis, ma'am. He say . . ." She paused and took a deep breath. "He say . . ."

"He say," Cody broke in, "old Dan Creek go to sleep and wake up dead!"

Spicy's hands dropped from Cassie's shoulders. "Dan gone?" she whispered as if she were sharing a secret with someone who was not there.

"Oh, no! He not going nowhere, Miz Davis." Cody scratched the back of one leg with a bare foot. "He laying right there all cold and dead in his cabin, man say."

"I go right down. You girls run home. Ask your mama if you can come over and stay with Rap 'til I get back. Come, honey, we go home."

"Dan really dead?" Rap whispered as he and Spicy hurried down the road. "He past and gone like my daddy."

"He gone," Aunt Spicy said firmly. "He not past. Not as long as we remember."

"That Jesse Creek. He didn't do anything bad, did he? He didn't hurt Dan?"

"No, boy." Spicy's words came out so slowly Rap had to connect them together himself. "I don't have . . . no time for that Jesse Creek. But . . . he wouldn't harm . . . his own daddy."

Rap sat alone on the porch steps waiting for Cassie and Cody. He tried to remember how Dan Creek looked, but the face blurred and all he could see was the old faded overalls.

One thing he knew for sure. He'd never go fishing again down by Dan's cabin! He'd never make another willow whistle either or climb the hickory or hunt crawdaddies or snare rabbits. He'd just forget Dan Creek and everything Dan ever taught him!

It was then he started to cry.

EIGHT

The sweetness of an Oklahoma June settled over the hills and spread across the valley. Mrs. Crumpton finally dismissed school for the summer. Days were long and lush and lazy, evenings soft and slow.

Aunt Spicy shooed Rap out of the house one morning. "Don't want you underfoot. I starting my spring house cleaning."

Rap knew very well it wasn't spring house cleaning. Aunt Spicy was starting to pack for Athabasca. The Toleses and Murphys had left the week before—two whole freight cars it took to carry their farm stuff, and everybody else who was planning on leaving Clearview were only waiting for the final word on the special train Reverend Sneed had ordered—a whole train with freight cars, passenger cars, engine, caboose—a whole train with no one else on it but Clearview folks bound for Athabasca.

Rap stood on the front porch with the world and the day spread out before him. When he was sitting in school and supposed to pay attention to Mrs. Crumpton, he could think of hundreds of things to do, but now nothing was exciting enough to begin, and with Jesse Creek hanging around Dan's cabin, Aunt Spicy had said, "You keep shut of that place."

He started down the road toward town, stopping long enough to throw rocks at a fence post. He missed.

"Hey, there. You Miss Davis' boy?"

A matched team, sleek and trim, leather harness gleaming, pulled up beside Rap.

"Yes, sir," Rap answered.

It was Sam Kelly and his canvas-covered wagon with the black and gold lettering, *Kelly's Liniments and Spices*, on the side.

Mr. Kelly always called on Aunt Spicy when he made his rounds, opening up his black suitcases in the kitchen and filling the room with warm smells of cinnamon and ginger and vanilla mixed in with the sweetness of camphor and lanolin.

"Could use some help. Could you use some money? Lot of new folks moved in here last few weeks. Could you show me around? Like the Fletchers. Got an order to deliver and can't find them."

"Fletchers took over Nimrod Toles's place. Toles, he went to Athabasca."

Mr. Kelly grinned down at Rap. "You ain't going to make any money giving away information free. Give you fifteen cents if you'll ride with me. Show me where these folks live. That be all right?"

Rap looked at the horses and the fancy wagon. "That be all right."

"Hop up, then." The man moved over. "But if we're going to be business partners today, I best know your name.

"I be A. J. Davis. Everybody call me Rap."

"I'll call you A. J. Fifteen cents. Shall we shake?"

Mr. Kelly extended his hand. It was white—white all over with a fuzz of reddish hair fringing the knuckles. Rap put out his hand. He had never touched a white man before—ever.

Rap watched the white hands pick up the shiny black reins. Dan Creek was right. That country up north sure sucked the color right out.

"I don't know where everybody lives," Rap said. "But I know somebody who does. His daddy owns the newspaper and he got a map of where everybody's been buying and moving in. We get back to town, I hire him. He part of my overhead."

Mr. Kelly looked over at Rap. "I think I've found me one smart partner."

"His name Lacey. His daddy own almost everything in Clearview."

"You talking about Jackson?"

"Yes, sir. Mr. Jackson."

"Good man, Jackson. 'Fraid he's losing out, though. These here towns like Clearview and Boley and the rest of them . . . they aren't going to last. Don't think setting up black towns and white towns is the way. 'Nother ten, twenty years there'll be nothing but weeds growing up and down their main streets, and it won't matter then what color the towns were."

"Aunt Spicy and me going to Athabasca. We not staying here."

Sam Kelly settled back in the seat and let the horses take up the slack in the reins. Rap sat up tall. The wagon wheels spewed out little puffs of dust as they wound around the base of High Hill and off toward the Toles farm.

"Want half?" Mr. Kelly held out a stick of candy.

"Sure."

The man snapped a dull yellow stick in two.

"Best candy made, this horehound."

Rap popped his half into his mouth. The taste was strange: sweet like too strong sorghum molasses, but as bitter as medicine.

"Like it?"

Rap shook his head.

"Me neither. Spit it out. Got a whole box of the stuff. Can't sell a stick of it."

"Maybe if you went into folks' houses sucking on it as if you liked it, folks'd buy. Aunt Spicy peddle her sour plums that way."

Mr. Kelly chuckled. "Never thought of that. We'll try it out on these Fletchers. You can't keep your mouth puckered up like that if we expect to peddle it, though."

The Fletchers bought ten sticks of horehound candy at two sticks for a penny. "I cut the price a bit, A.J.," the drummer confided as they rode back toward town. "Doesn't pay to take too much advantage of a customer. Now you say this friend of yours can get us a map?"

"Sure."

"Where will we find him?"

"Oh, he be hanging around his daddy's office or down at the depot someplace."

They didn't have to find Lacey. Lacey found them. As soon as Mr. Kelly pulled his rig up in front of the newspaper office, there was Lacey, hightailing it across the schoolhouse yard.

"For a nickel?" Lacey looked up at the wagon.

"That's what I said, a nickel," Rap repeated.

"White man paying you?"

"Mr. Kelly pay me."

"Map'll cost three cents more." Lacey fingered

his watch chain that drooped from his belt over to his pocket.

"Offer him three sticks for his map," Mr. Kelly called from the wagon seat.

"How about it?" Rap insisted. "Five cents and three sticks of candy and I'll sit in the middle and you can ride on the outside."

The bargain was made.

Mr. Kelly guided the rig out across the valley, Lacey pointing the way from farm to farm.

"You and your daddy going up to this Athabasca?" Mr. Kelly propped his feet up against the wagon rail, leaned back, letting the horses set their own pace.

"We staying here," Lacey mumbled. "We going to watch Clearview grow. My daddy, he in Texas right now getting more folks to come up."

"Your daddy picked a hard row to hoe. Texas folks coming to Clearview. Clearview folks leaving for Athabasca. Like pouring water into a bucket with holes in the bottom. Got to be fast on your feet to keep a bucket like that full."

"My daddy, he don't worry. He say after one winter up there in Athabasca everybody'll be coming back anyway."

"Will not," Rap argued. "We be up there on free land and you be down here with Jim Crow on your shoulder. We do anything we want. Nobody tell us what to do. Won't be any school, even, 'cause Mrs. Crumpton's not going."

"Well . . ." Mr. Kelly yawned. "Don't want to take sides in this dispute, but I hope you're right, Lacey. I'd be out of business if these towns like Clearview and Boley fold. Of course, if there's somebody coming in to buy up the land, things should stay about the same."

"My daddy selling land all the time." Lacey turned to Rap. "Bet you didn't know he sell your Aunt Spicy's place last night. You'll have to go now 'cause you not got a place to live no more."

"Don't believe you." It was one thing to be selling. It was another to have Spicy's place already sold. "Who bought it?"

"That Jesse Creek. One with the big car. He going out to see your Aunt Spicy today."

"You making that up. Thought your daddy only sell to colored folks. Jesse Creek, he Indian."

Lacey squinted off across the fields. "Sometimes, Rap Davis, seems like you don't know nothing. Jesse Creek *part* Indian, *part* colored. My daddy sold your Aunt Spicy's place to the colored part of him."

"Now me," Mr. Kelly broke in. "I don't give a hoot about anybody's color. Know why, A.J.?" He nudged Rap. " 'Cause no matter whether they be red or black or white or yellow, all their money's silver."

It was late afternoon by the time they drove back into Clearview, Mr. Kelly's pocket full of jingling coins.

"Wonder what's up." He pointed to the depot where a crowd of people were gathered as if it were Excursion Days over again, but they weren't getting on or off a train this time. They were reading something posted on the wall of the depot.

"Well, A.J.," the man said as he pulled the team to a stop. "I'll drop you and your friend off here. Here's what I owe you. You pay off Lacey there."

Rap and Lacey climbed down from the wagon

and raced toward the depot, elbowing their way through the crowd. It was hard to see what was printed on the poster. Everyone was so much taller and the notice wasn't very big:

**SPECIAL TRAIN FOR ATHABASCA
DUE JUNE 16-8 AM
ACCOMMODATIONS FOR 200
SPECIAL CARS FOR HOUSE-
HOLD GOODS AND FARM EQUIPMENT
SIGN UP WITH REVEREND SNEED**

"We really going!" shouted Rap, turning toward Lacey, but Lacey was gone. Rap shoved his way back through the crowd. "Hey, Lacey! You read it!"

Lacey didn't answer. He was trudging across the schoolhouse yard, hands jammed deep into his pockets, shoulders bent as though he were carrying something heavy on his back. Lacey hadn't even asked for his nickel.

With the money in his pocket, Rap ran toward home. He'd be the first to tell Aunt Spicy, unless she'd already been to town and seen the notice.

Cassie and Cody met him at the crossroads.

"We leaving for Athabasca next week," Cassie shouted. "We already packing."

"We already packing," Cody echoed.

First thing Rap knew, they had him by the hands dancing him around in a dizzy circle.

"Mama's making me a new dress to wear on the train. It be blue."

"New dress," Cody repeated.

Rap tried hard to look grown-up, but the next thing he knew he was shouting too:

Mrs. Mac, Mac, Mac
Dressed in black, black, black
Athabasca, Athabasca
Down her back, back, back.

Around and around they went until Cody stumbled and pulled them all down in a dusty, laughing heap.

"Cody and me's going to go up and down the train even while it be moving."

"We going to play games all day and all night." It was the first time Rap had ever heard Cody make a sentence of her own.

"I got to go!" Rap scrambled to his feet. "Got to tell Aunt Spicy."

He ran all the way home, but stopped short on the front porch. Voices stopped him, not so much because they were loud, but because they were so fierce.

"Too late now, Jesse Creek," Aunt Spicy almost shouted. "You ain't got no claim."

"Mine by rights!" Jesse Creek's voice cut like a knife.

"Ten years late. Where was you when me and my sister had to tend to everything?"

"Trying to live. I got a little money now. I want a place. I paid."

"Paid! You paid money. Think you can take my place with money? I paid ten years of my life."

"Good ten years, weren't they? What did I have? Nothing. Nobody."

"You made your choice long time ago. You can't show up here now and change things."

Rap knew buying and selling were important, but he didn't know folks argued about it when it was done. Aunt Spicy was sure wearing her mean shoes with that Jesse Creek! Maybe she wanted more money for her place.

"I'm not changing nothing." Jesse's voice was low. "You are doing the changing. Picking up and leaving."

"Leaving! Anybody who knows leaving be you! Only trouble, you should have stayed away. Take your daddy. He didn't leave. He helped. He didn't go around like some puppy with his tail 'tween his legs. Your daddy a man. That's more than you ever been except once."

It was quiet for so long that Rap thought they were all through. Listening to the silence was worse than hearing the words.

"Spicy," Jesse's voice was so different, Rap could have believed that it was somebody else talking. "I was young. Mixed-up. Almost crazy."

"I know that. So were we all." Aunt Spicy's voice was softer, but just as strong. "But when it comes right down to it, you're asking too much. I earned what I got. I going to keep it."

It was quiet again, and Rap felt as if he could almost hear Jesse scrambling for something to say.

The screen door opened slowly, and Jesse Creek backed out, closing the door gently. "Spicy." He spoke through the screen door. "You always was a strong, righteous woman, but righteous don't mean right. It's not finished yet."

He turned and walked down the porch steps, not even glancing at Rap.

That mean Jesse Creek! Always hanging around, making trouble! And now just because he had a wallet full of money, he had to come upsetting Aunt Spicy.

Rap didn't want to go into the room where the echo of the angry words still hung in the air. He walked slowly around the house. Aunt Spicy was sitting on a stump out by the chicken coop, staring up at High Hill as if she expected something to come sailing over the top. She was always on the move, talking, cooking, cleaning, choring, and to see her now all still and quiet was scary.

Rap walked up behind her and stopped. She looked so little sitting there. It was almost like the older he got, the smaller she grew. Maybe it was because she worked so hard all the time, just like she'd told Jesse Creek, earning her place.

Rap had earned something too. The three nickels lay smooth and cool in his pants pocket.

"Aunt Spicy." His voice sounded funny, even to him. "I got three nickels. Helped Mr. Kelly. Won't let Jessie Creek take nothing from you."

Spicy looked down at the three coins, stood up slowly and without saying a word, put her arms around his shoulders, pulled him close, pressing his nose into her neck. "Honey." He could feel her lips move against his ear. "I got me a real man, ten years old or not."

NINE

"**O**ne week to pack and 'liquefy' our assets," Aunt Spicy announced as she sorted through a pile of Rap's clothes. "I know the word is liquidate, but I like 'liquefy' better 'cause what we doing is boiling things down to what we take on the train."

The boiling down meant selling most of the jars of food in the cave, dickering with the Fletchers over a price for the pigs and Old Bones and one of her calves.

"We take one calf so we can start our herd up there. We sell all the chickens, though, for our nest egg." Aunt Spicy chuckled.

That was when Rap began to feel bad: when the mean old rooster was pushed into the crate and the produce wagon rumbled off down the road with the rooster's head stretched out between the slats of the crate. It didn't get any better when Aunt Spicy said the night before they were to leave, "Best take a last look around, boy. We leaving tomorrow morning early."

High Hill glowed golden in the setting sun as he cut across the pasture, hurried past the big hickory, ran over the crest of the hill and down to Salt

Creek. He hadn't started out to go to Dan Creek's cabin. He didn't want to run into that Jesse Creek again, but something tugged him along the familiar path.

He stopped at the edge of the clearing. He thought he heard a movement in the brush. He dropped down in the weeds and waited. Nothing moved. He stood up and crept up to the cabin. The door was half open. A big, black and yellow spider sat in the middle of a web that stretched across the opening. He didn't look inside, but sat down on the bottom step. Dan's chair was gone from its place against the cabin wall, but there was the same bare spot where Dan's shoes had scuffed away the grass, and holes still sunk into the ground from the chair legs.

"I come down to see you, Dan," Rap said aloud, making like Dan was sitting in the same old chair up against the cabin. "How come you didn't hear me?"

It wasn't hard to talk. Every summer day of his life he'd come down to the cabin and talk to Dan, and most of the time the old man just sat and listened and never said a word.

"We going to Athabasca, Dan. Best thing about it, there ain't no school. I write you a letter . . . draw pictures of what it's like, maybe. Bet someday you could get on a train and come up and we could go fishing. When I get bigger, I come back and see you. Tell you all about Eskimos and fat fish."

A flock of crows cawed their way from Smollett's cornfield and settled down in the trees behind the cabin.

"Best go now. Aunt Spicy be waiting. I take my

fishing line along, if you don't mind. Might be a lot of fish all the way up north."

He reached under the steps and found his hook and line. Carefully he wound it into a neat coil and slipped it into his pocket with his granddaddy's knife.

Near dusk, the special train whistled its way into Clearview.

"Can we go down and see it?" Rap climbed up on the top rail of the porch, watching the smoke from the engine drift like a black cloud over the town.

"Can't board tonight. You see plenty of that train before we get where we're going."

Rap couldn't sleep. The house was empty of furniture. Spicy had sold all but one bed and a dresser, and they were crated and down at the depot ready to be loaded along with the boxes of household things. He and Spicy shared a pillow and blanket on the bare floor. The wagons rumbled by all night, loaded with plows and harrows and seeders and after the wagons came the bawls and grunts of livestock being driven to the depot.

The empty house creaked and rustled with strange noises, and the windows stared like blank eyes into the dark. Spicy claimed that whenever folks moved out of a house, their spirits stayed on. Rap wasn't sure he wanted his spirit hanging around a house that Jesse Creek was going to live in. Of course if Spicy's spirit hung around too, it would be all right being in two places at once. That way he wouldn't have to leave Clearview really. Leaving any place wasn't much fun unless it was school and even thinking about never sitting there in front of Mrs. Crumpton again wasn't so good either.

He didn't think he slept at all, but Spicy, the next morning, claimed he was asleep as soon as his head hit the pillow.

The depot platform swarmed with people. Folks hurried excitedly to board the train while others who were staying lined up against the depot wall, shaking their heads, muttering, "They'll be sorry. You see."

Aunt Spicy, a basket of carefully packed necessities hooked over her arm, tugged Rap through the crowd. Spicy maintained there were only two things needed in life: food and a change of underwear.

Reverend Sneed stood on one of the depot benches checking off the departing families and booming out directions in his best preaching voice. The Mapps lined up, waiting to get on board, Cassie in her new blue dress and Cody in a matching pink.

"That's our car," Spicy said, setting down her basket. "You wait here. I say goodby to Granny Carson and I must see Mrs. Crumpton before we leave."

Rap was glad Aunt Spicy had told him to wait. He didn't want to get on the train quite yet. He looked out across the valley toward High Hill and followed the thread of road that ran down past the church, the school, until it became Main Street. He closed his eyes to see if he could remember exactly the way it looked. He didn't want to forget, ever.

Someone shoved him so hard in the back that he almost fell over. He spun around and there stood

Lacey acting as if he didn't know anything about someone being shoved.

"Came down to say goodby," he said, not looking at Rap.

"Didn't think your daddy'd let you."

"My daddy say he didn't care, 'cause you'd all be back soon enough. Daddy say they stopping trains at the Canada border. You never get there."

"I not afraid. Besides your daddy don't know everything."

"He say by the time you get back we have a glove factory here, a couple of mines, a new school, and a college even. Clearview going to grow to be the biggest city in Okfuskee County. You just see."

"Everything down here going to cost. Where we going it's free. I write you all about it. You can write me. Mr. A. J. Davis, Athabasca, Canada."

Lacey gave him another shove, not so hard this time. "Going to miss your dumb old face, Rap. Got something for you." He unfastened the chain from his belt loop and held out his watch.

"You giving this to me?"

"Yah."

"Your daddy be mad."

"Naw. Buy me another. Besides this one don't work. Never did."

"How come you always looking at it?"

"I make like it works. You make like something's real, it's real."

The watch was smooth in Rap's hand, polished like the stones he used to find in the creek down by old Dan's cabin.

"You giving me the chain too?"

"Sure." Lacey rocked back on his heels. "But

you owe me a nickel. Remember? For helping Mr. Kelly."

"I know." Rap reached in his pocket. It was the same nickel Lacey had given him for putting up the Excursion Day signs. Spicy had saved it for him in the cupboard.

"Bet you wouldn't have given it to me less I asked."

"Would too, Lacey." Rap dropped the coin into the outstretched palm. "You my best friend."

"I got to go now." Lacey's voice got funny. He slipped the coin in his pocket, turned, dashed through the crowd, jumped the three steps down from the depot platform, and broke into a run, not once looking back.

Far down the track the engine belched out a puff of steam and the train cars shuddered and banged together. Above the voices, the locomotive's bell clanged.

"All right, folks," called Reverend Sneed. "Everybody on board. We leaving right soon!"

Aunt Spicy emerged from the crowd, grabbed Rap by the arm, and herded him down the track to their car.

"Watch your step, lady," a man warned as he helped Aunt Spicy step on a little stool and then up the iron steps into the train.

"Spicy!" Jesse Creek's voice stopped her on the top step. "Wait a minute."

Spicy turned and looked down at him. "Waiting time ran out ten years ago, Jesse Creek, when you made that promise."

"You made one too." Jesse leaned across the steps blocking Rap from following Spicy.

"Yes, and I'll keep it. We both wait and see what

happens. You can't have everything." She turned and walked into the train.

"Not everything. Just my share," he shouted after her.

Rap started up the steps.

"So, Anson J. You're off to Athabasca."

"Yes, sir. But I got to go now. Aunt Spicy be waiting."

"You take good care of your Aunt Spicy, you hear?" Jesse Creek looked at him so hard Rap's ears burned. "And listen to what she has to tell you."

"Yes, sir." Rap hurried up the steps, then turned. "Mr. Creek. If anybody ask. That name in the storm cave. That be mine."

The train car was wider than Aunt Spicy's house and longer than the Pentecostal Church. Aunt Spicy had already found them a seat. The train lurched and started to move. Rap held on with both hands. Then the whole world began to move, slowly at first, then faster and faster, past Mrs. Doggett's store, Atkins Hotel, Erving's Emporium, and as the train whistle blew three long blasts, they flew across the road that wound out of town toward Okmulgee.

Standing at the crossing was Lacey Jackson, waving like crazy. Rap tried to wave back, but the train was going too fast.

TEN

Athabasca was more than a word, now, more than a song, more than a where. Athabasca was a dream coming real.

The Oklahoma countryside flew past as the train picked up speed, changing shrubs and trees into blurs of greens and browns, pushing telegraph poles into picket fences, melting the cinder roadbed into a flowing river of black.

Face pressed against the window, Rap felt as if the train were standing still and the land sliding past to the rhythm of iron wheels on steel rails clicking out, "Athabasca. Athabasca. Athabasca. Athabasca."

They screamed through a little town and before Rap could blink, they were whistling out into the country again with whole pastures and fields flying by as if they were gardens.

"You get sick, boy, looking out that window all the time," Aunt Spicy said, resting her head back against the plush seat and stretching out her legs. "Turn your stomach upside down."

"Didn't know Athabasca be so far," Rap marveled.

"Far? We ain't even started, honey. Athabascas take time for getting to."

"Someday I go back to Clearview, maybe." Rap turned from the window.

"Maybe you will. Who's to say?" Spicy said, her eyes closed.

Rap turned back to the window. The world was so big. How could they be riding all morning and still be in Oklahoma? Aunt Spicy had shown him on a map where the thin lines of railroad tracks slashed up through Missouri and Iowa and Minnesota and on into Canada. Aunt Spicy's map stopped just past the border.

Canada? A shadow grew in the back of his mind. He was leaving Clearview. He was leaving Oklahoma. He was leaving the United States!

"Aunt Spicy, what we be in Athabasca?"

"What we always be," Spicy answered, her eyes still closed.

"Not American no more?"

"No. 'Fraid we give up on America."

"I be a Canada man then?"

"Canadian."

"I learn all that old history stuff about America for nothing?"

"We make new history in Athabasca. You and me. You see."

Aunt Spicy slept, her flowered hat held carefully in her lap. After all the excitement of leaving, folks had quieted down except for a cough or a baby's cry. Mrs. Crumpton was sure going to be mad in the fall. Most everybody in her whole school was on the train except for Lacey. The trouble was they were either older or younger. He was awfully glad Cassie was along; of course he'd never tell her. He hadn't seen her since they boarded the train. He could go and look for her, but he didn't want to wake Aunt Spicy by crawling across and he didn't dare leave his window for fear he might miss something important. It was like somebody out there was flipping pictures at him so fast that just when he fixed his eyes on one thing, it was gone and there was something new to see. Lacey Jackson didn't know what he was missing.

He was beginning to get hungry, really hungry, when Aunt Spicy woke, put on her hat, and reached under the seat for her basket of necessities. "Got all our eatings in these little bundles. Enough to get us to St. Paul. We stop there for more."

The fried chicken and homemade bread spattered with chunks of cold butter tasted so good that Rap took tiny little bites to make it last.

"That's all you get 'til supper," Aunt Spicy ordered. "Now, if you thirsty, take this cup and walk down the aisle clear down to the end of the car. Stone crock there, up on the wall. Turn the handle at the bottom, and you'll get your drink."

Rap took the tin cup and started down the aisle. At first he didn't know what had happened. Maybe it was because he had been sitting at the window so long his legs had forgotten how to walk. He didn't think he'd ever sat still so long before, longer even than Mrs. Crumpton's study periods. He took one step and bumped into the seat across the aisle. He grabbed to steady himself; but was thrown against the opposite seat. It was like trying to swim upstream in Salt Creek. He zigzagged down the length of the car, like one of the big Smolletts when he got too much homebrew.

Everything was changing so fast, Rap couldn't

keep track: the motion of the train beneath his feet, the world outside the train, even the water. Water ought to taste like water no matter where he was, and this didn't except it was wet.

As he turned to go back with a drink for Aunt Spicy, Cassie, with Cody close behind, came down the aisle careening from seat to seat.

"You been yet?" Cassie giggled.

"Been where?"

Cassie clapped her hand over her mouth.

"You know." Cody spoke out all on her own. "The Where-You-Have-to-Go-Place."

"It's right here on the train." Cassie giggled. "We carrying it along with us!"

"Inside," Code exclaimed, her eyes wide.

If it had been Lacey Jackson's story, Rap never would have believed it.

"You got to go look," Cassie whispered. "Even if you don't have to go."

"If you pull the handle"—Cody shivered—"see the ground moving!"

"Look down through the place, and the ground swishes past under," Cassie added. "More fun than looking out the window. Go see. It's clear down at the other end. And there's one in every car!"

"How'd you get in this car!"

"It's real scary. You open a door and in this little place there's an iron board to walk across and you can see the wheels and the ground moving under and then there's another door and you're in the next car. We go through the whole train. We do it again. Want to come?"

"Sure. I take this drink to Aunt Spicy and ask her."

"Don't ask." Cassie giggled again. "Say you got to go."

"Well, go then," Aunt Spicy agreed. "You can't get lost. And mind you don't bother folks."

Cassie led them through all five passenger cars as far as they could go until they got to the freight cars; then they turned and went all the way back to the very last car, just before the caboose. The worst part was stepping across the metal platform between cars, where it felt as if one more shake of the train and they'd all tumble through the cracks and get chewed up by the grinding wheels.

By the time Rap got back, he really did have to go, but not with Cassie and Cody standing outside the door.

"I got to talk to Aunt Spicy now. Tell her how things is." Rap tried to look as if he had important private things to say. "I come up where you be later. Maybe we play a game."

The Where-You-Have-to-Go-Place was every bit as marvelous as Cassie had said.

They slept that night, Rap with his head cushioned in Aunt Spicy's lap, and she sitting upright, her feet propped up on her basket. At dawn, Rap wakened.

"Something wrong, Aunt Spicy," he whispered, tugging at her arm. "We stop. We in Athabasca?"

Aunt Spicy opened her eyes slowly, turned to look out the window, glanced across the aisle at the other sleeping passengers and replied, "We off on a siding."

"Why we sitting here?"

"We wait for trains to come by. See, honey,

there just one track, and we take our turns. It not our turn yet."

All morning the train sat on the siding. Finally Reverend Sneed opened the door of the car. "Brothers and sisters. Seems we will be sitting here for another hour or so. We just a little ways from Iowa border. Engineer say if you want to get out and stretch your legs, it be all right. When we ready to move again, he'll pull the whistle."

Rap dodged down the aisle.

"Mind now. Don't stray too far," Aunt Spicy called after him. "And don't get into any trouble."

The heat shimmered up in waves from the cindered track. The grass along the road bed was burnt and withered and trees fringing the town drooped in the hot sun.

"Hey, Rap!" Cassie called. "We go up and look at the engine. Man say they going to take on water from a big tank."

"Train don't run on water. Train run on fire."

"How you think they make steam, Rap Davis? Mix up fire and water and make steam and that's how trains run. I read all about it in a book Mrs. Crumpton give me."

They ran down the track, Rap marveling at the size of the iron wheels.

"Four. Five. Six. Seven," Cassie counted as she raced toward the engine. "Seven freight cars and five people cars and look at that!"

The engine towered high above them, black and sleek and powerful, with an engineer leaning back in the cab, one elbow stuck out the window. "Stay back, you hear?" He motioned. "Taking on water and don't need nobody getting hurt."

They edged back and watched. A man in a striped

cap climbed up on top of the locomotive, crawled along, stood up, and reached for a rope dangling down from a tin chute. Beyond the chute loomed a steel tank propped up on four iron legs and as big around as a house.

"That tank full of water!" Rap exclaimed as a stream gushed down the chute and into the engine.

"They's already loaded the coal on. Me and Cody saw them," Cassie boasted.

"We saw them," echoed Cody.

"And up there's the depot. Cody and me's not been there yet. Want to go?"

"Sure," Rap agreed. "We go look."

The loading platform was empty, but a man in shirt sleeves and a funny green cap pulled down to shade his eyes sat in a little room that jutted out from the depot like Lacey Jackson's fancy front window.

"He the telegraph man," Cassie explained as if she were leading a tour.

"This depot sure bigger than Clearview's. Not as new, though," Rap observed.

"Let's go inside," Cassie urged. "It's hot out here."

"Hot," Cody agreed.

They peered through the screen door into the cool darkness.

"Look at those benches!"

They were long, long as half a railroad car, and made of slick, shiny wood, polished like glass.

"Bet we could start at one end . . ." Cassie began.

"And slide clear down to the other end on our bottoms," Cody finished.

"Don't see no people in there," Rap said, cupping his hands around his eyes and staring through the screen.

They were three steps inside the door when a deep voice spoke sternly from behind a caged window. "You're in the wrong place."

Rap stopped so suddenly that Cody almost knocked him over from behind.

"Your place," the man went on, "is around back."

Rap's stomach tightened. The man sounded as if he were reciting words he had memorized, and though he was looking at them, it was as if they had already left.

Cassie sidled up to Rap. "He must be talking to us," she whispered. "Ain't nobody else in here."

One by one they edged out the door onto the hot platform.

"He say our place 'round back," Cody puzzled. "And he don't even know us!"

"Bet this for grownups. We go look at the round-back place," Cassie said eagerly. "Maybe it special for us kids."

They raced around the corner of the depot. Rap saw the door first and then the sign. They stood, faces tilted up.

"I could print better than that when I was five," Rap finally said, his mouth dry. "They got the 'r' backward in *colored*."

"Don't like this place," Cody whimpered.

"Me neither," Rap muttered.

Cassie turned without looking at either of them. "We go back to our train."

Together, they walked slowly down the black-cindered track.

Rap did not turn his head to watch the world go past as the train churned slowly toward the north.

"You hungry?" Aunt Spicy asked, reaching for her basket.

"No, ma'am."

Not until it was dark and the stars made their own bright patterns in the sky did Rap stare out into the night.

"You feel all right, boy?" Aunt Spicy turned to look down at him.

His mouth tried to shape the words. Then they came while he listened to his own question. "Why didn't you tell me?"

"Why didn't I tell you what?"

"That whites got places for us 'round back."

Aunt Spicy sat very still for a long time; then she drew in a deep breath, put her arm around Rap, and nestled him in the crook of her elbow as if he were a baby. The train rocked gently through the summer night, whistling as it passed through darkened towns.

"I know everybody ain't alike, Aunt Spicy. But how come being different makes a difference?"

ELEVEN

Aunt Spicy never did answer his question—just held him until he went to sleep, and then, when he woke the next morning, she talked about everything else so he couldn't find a place to ask again. The more he thought, the more he decided that was Aunt Spicy's way: throwing him scraps that never answered anything and telling him he'd find out everything soon enough by himself.

Lacey Jackson sure wasn't missing nothing. The train was as bad as the pendulum on Mrs. Crumpton's schoolroom clock, moving from side to side and not getting nowhere, and now they were stopped again, swallowed up in a tunnel of green trees.

"Bridge out, folks say. Probably be here a pretty spell," Aunt Spicy explained.

"Where's here?"

"Boone County. Des Moines River off there some place. We in Iowa."

"Sure have funny names." Rap watched a squirrel run up the trunk of a maple and swing across to another as if he had wings. "Not easy names like Weleetka or Okmulgee or Okfuskee."

103

The door at the end of the car clanged open, and Reverend Sneed raised his arms as if he were going to say a blessing. "We all be sidetracked here for a day or two while they fix the washout up head. We going into the next town for food. Tonight we have an old-fashioned Clearview picnic here in the woods."

"I go find Cassie. We go exploring."

"Stay within hearing of the whistle," Aunt Spicy warned.

Rap ran down the side of the train, the cinders crunching like hot coals. "Cassie!" How wonderful to holler! "Cassie!" How wonderful to run!

"Cassie inside," Cody shouted as she dashed past.

"What she doing there?"

Cody was gone.

Rap climbed the iron steps and peeked around the deserted car. Slowly he walked down the aisle, looking from seat to seat. A pile of bed quilts turned out to be Cassie, scrunched up like a baby rabbit in a clump of grass.

"What you doing?"

Cassie peeked over the edge of the quilt, her eyes little slits. "I sick."

"Sick?"

"Cold and shivery."

"Can't be cold. It hot out."

"Just same, I cold."

Cassie's face, usually a soft black velvet, was splotched with gray. "Mama say I picked up an Iowa burning-bug."

"Ain't seen no bug around."

"Don't have to see one. Have to get one."

"Don't want none of your bugs. I going exploring. I come back. Tell you all about this Iowa. Maybe this afternoon your bugs be gone."

"I haven't got *bugs*, Rap Davis. I got *a* bug." Cassie snuggled deeper into the quilt and buried her head under both arms.

The Iowa woods weren't much different from the woods on High Hill, the trees taller, the underbrush thicker. He hadn't walked very far until all the voices from the train were blotted out and only the soft twitter of birds and a squirrel's chatter broke the heavy quiet. He walked carefully as Dan had taught him. He was afraid, but he thrust his hand in his pocket, his fingers curling around his grandpa's knife. Maybe he'd make himself a whistle. Willows ought to be growing down by the creek.

Aunt Spicy had warned him not to get lost, but Dan had told him no one could get lost in a woods if there was a creek to follow home.

Maybe he'd make two willow whistles and take one back to Cassie. He reached out to grab a branch when something thunked against the tree trunk behind him. He stood, arm still outstretched, unmoving, and slowly turned his head.

"Wasn't trying to hit you."

Squinting into the sun, Rap looked far up into the branches. A boy, perched high in the tree, looked down, his blond hair shining.

"What you aiming at then?"

"Squirrel. Would have had him too if you hadn't come along. You're so dark, I didn't see you. You from that black train?"

"Train not black. Engine black. Caboose red. Our car's yellow."

The boy's feet came down the tree first, then

overalled legs. He wasn't much bigger than Rap.
"I didn't mean the train was black. I meant the
people were black, like you."

"We colored."

Rap had never seen any one so white except for
the freckles splotched on his face.

"You got a name?"

"I be A. J. Davis. Who you?"

"Elmer. It's my pa's name too. Want to see my
slingshot?" The boy pulled a forked branch from
his back pocket, stretched the rubber straps almost to his ear and let fly a stone that bounced
among the trees.

"Want to try? Made it myself."

"Sure." Rap reached out to take the slingshot.

"Hey! It don't come off!" Elmer stared at Rap's
palm.

"What don't?"

"The black."

"Course not. Your freckles come off?"

"No, it's my skin."

"This be my skin too. How you keep the rock
in?"

"You got to hold it like this." Elmer stepped
behind Rap, reached over his shoulder, and covered Rap's hand with his own. "Hold tight to the
rock. Pull back and let go."

The rock whistled up through the trees, clipping
off leaves in its path.

"What you doing here? My pa owns these woods."

"Train stopped 'til they fix the bridge. I exploring. Going to make me some whistles."

"How you do that?"

"Thought everybody know how to make a whistle. Come on. I'll show you. You got a knife?"

"Naw. Lost it."

"Don't matter. We use mine."

They sat side by side in the dappled shade. Rap's whistle was done in no time. Elmer whittled, carved, tugged, and when he was finished, his whistle barely made a squawk.

"It ain't easy the first time, Elmer," Rap said. "See, when Dan Creek teach me, it took maybe three or four times before I got it right."

"Who's Dan Creek? Your pa?"

"Naw. He a Creek back in Oklahoma."

"How can someone be a creek?"

"They Indians. Creek Indians."

"Going to be more Indians where you're heading."

"How you know where we going?"

"Everybody 'round here knew you were coming through. Didn't know you were stopping. Why you going up there, anyway?"

"We starting a whole new town."

"I ain't going nowhere. Pa says next year I can quit school and help him."

"No school where I'm going."

They stalked rabbits through the brush. Elmer whipped out his slingshot and tried to stun a carp that hovered lazily in the still backwater of the creek. They climbed the tallest tree and saw the train stretched like an empty snake skin along the edge of the woods. Elmer borrowed Rap's knife and peeled the bark from a tree, stripping off a thin piece of the white inner layer.

"Chew it." Elmer grinned. "It's slippery elm. Keep chewing 'til the slippery's gone."

They were gathering branches when the train whistle sounded. Rap dropped his armful. "I got to go. We having a picnic."

"You can't go now," Elmer cried. "We ain't got our hideout built."

"I come back tomorrow. We finish it then."

Elmer dropped his branches on the pile. "You promise? I'll get here early. Want to borrow my slingshot? You can practice. Give it back to me in the morning."

Rap took the slingshot and slipped it into his back pocket. "I'll trade you my watch." Rap unhooked the chain and held it out. "It don't work. Stuck on twelve, but you can make like it's any time you want it to be."

Elmer linked the chain around his overall strap and tucked the watch into the pocket on his chest. "See you in the morning then. Don't forget."

"I won't forget," Rap promised.

Rap was out of breath when he got back. A spiral of smoke curled up from across the tracks and the smell of roasting pork hung in the evening air. The clearing beside the tracks was black with people, men standing around the fire while women spread out tablecloths and children darted in and out among the grownups. Mr. Mapp sat, his back against a tree stump, his hands cupped around a harmonica, his foot tapping time to his music.

Rap ran down the track and climbed into the train, the slingshot in his hand. "Cassie," he shouted, running down the aisle.

Aunt Spicy's head rose above the seat. "Hush, boy. Cassie's sleeping."

"What's wrong with her?"

"She got fevers and chills."

"She going to miss all the fun."

"Keep back. Don't want you catching her bug. I stay with her tonight. Reverend Sneed say weather so good, everybody sleep outside. You fetch your pillow and quilt and if you need anything, ask Mrs. Sneed."

"Where's Cassie's mama?"

"She got her hands full taking care of the other little ones. Don't want them coming down with the same bug."

Rap tiptoed out of the car.

"Everybody gather 'round now after you fill your plate," boomed Reverend Sneed.

The fire glowed red in the fading light, casting shadows across the clearing, mingling with the blink of lightning bugs from the nearby woods.

"We got a farmer to thank for the meat we's eating. Saved us a long walk into town. He say town up head ain't too happy to have us here." Reverend Sneed looked off into the woods. "Don't expect no trouble, but think the men folks best sleep with one eye open tonight. But ain't no need to spoil our evening."

After supper, the singing started and went on into the night. Mrs. Sneed found Rap a place by the dying fire to spread out his quilt, and he tucked the slingshot under his pillow and stared up into the night sky.

The stars looked so close he could almost reach out and touch them, like lightning bugs flying beyond his reach. Folks weren't singing loud now, only humming the words without really saying them. Over the treetops hung a star, brighter than all the rest. If Cassie were around, she'd know its name.

What if there were a boy just like him on that star looking down the same time he was looking up? And this boy would be wondering the same thing Rap was, and maybe there'd even be an Athabasca or some place like it there. What would the boy look like? Like Elmer? What if folks there were one color. Gold, maybe.

The firelight and the singing and the star faded and Rap was standing on top of a high hill in Athabasca and Elmer was running toward him swinging Lacey's silver watch.

A long, drawn-out whistle broke through the stillness of the early dawn. An owl hooted and swooped off, leaves rustling as if a wind had passed over the treetops.

Reverend Sneed emerged from the shadows of the train. "Track's clear! We're moving out! Everybody back on the train!"

"You awake?" Mrs. Sneed bent over Rap, looming like a big cloud of mist in her long white nightgown. "Pick up your covers and get to your car. Your Aunt Spicy still with Cassie."

Eyes half-closed, Rap stumbled up the steps and down the dark aisle. He propped his pillow against the window, snuggled under his quilt, and stretched out across the two seats. He flopped over on his side, tucking his hands under the pillow.

The slingshot! He'd forgotten to pick it up. This was tomorrow and they were leaving. He wouldn't be able to trade back for Lacey's watch. That didn't matter. He'd rather have the slingshot anyway. *It* worked.

He hurried off the train and ran toward the glow of the fire. On hands and knees he searched through the grass. The engine, far down the track, sounded like some big animal, panting and moaning and stirring in its sleep. Iron door clanged. Voices shouted orders.

Frantically he hunted. He had to get the sling-shot. What if Elmer came back and found it? He'd think Rap had thrown it away. The train lurched forward, clanged to a stop, then ground backwards, brakes grinding.

His hand closed over the smooth wood of Elmer's slingshot, but before he could get to his feet, the train started moving ahead, picking up speed, and slipping down the track faster than he could run. He stood, slingshot in hand, and watched the red light of the caboose blink and fade away.

TWELVE

Far down the tracks, the train whistled again. Rap felt as if half of him were stretched out on the seat, his head on the pillow, while the other half stood alone in the clearing, the camp fire dying at his feet.

Folks on the train wouldn't even miss him! Aunt Spicy was back with Cassie. Mrs. Sneed would think he was sleeping under his quilt. His sides ached as if he had been running and his head felt as empty as the clearing.

He could follow the track, but it stretched like a dark tunnel between trees. He could hide, but there was nothing to hide from. He could stay where he was and hope the train would back up when they missed him.

He thought longingly of Aunt Spicy's basket of necessities, but he had necessities: a fishline, a knife, a slingshot. Old Dan had told him all he ever needed in the woods was a way to make a fire and a way to get food. He felt better already, as if he weren't alone.

He'd start the fire again. He ran to the edge of the woods and gathered twigs. The embers caught with a crackle. He hurried to bank the fire with two half-rotted logs. He would wait until full daylight, then he would start down the track.

With his granddaddy's knife, he dug around in the soft spot where the logs had rested until he had half a dozen fat, white grubs. There would be fish back in the stream where Elmer had tried to hit the carp. He'd catch him a fish, have breakfast, and start walking to Athabasca.

He felt safer in the woods, making like he was in the timber back on High Hill with the creek cutting a black path through the underbrush. He baited his hook and huddled under an elderberry bush that drooped over into the water. The sky toward the east glowed pink. He clutched his line and whispered softly as Dan had taught him, "Brother Fish. Brother Fish."

From behind, he heard muffled shouts.

Had they discovered he was missing? Stopped the train? Come back to get him?

He started to pull in his line as the voices came nearer; then a man shouted from downstream, "No coons left! Got away."

"Told you we waited too long," came an answer. "Catch coons ya have to do it in the dark."

"How you find them?" someone else called back. "Can't see them in the dark."

"Whites of their eyes, man."

Coon hunters. But coon hunters had dogs. Rap didn't hear any dogs. He crept farther back under the bush.

"They been around, though," another voice called. "Still smell them. Once you've smelled one, you can't mistake one."

"Hell! We missed some good fun. Sure liked to have sent them napheads on their way."

The men were not talking about raccoons! Rap pulled his knees up and crawled farther back into the darkness of the bush.

Someone crashed through the timber, stopped beside the elderberry bush, and in a voice Rap knew shouted, "This is where they were, Pa, but I told you they'd be gone. Didn't you hear the train whistle?"

An older voice answered, "Dammit, boy! Your fault we didn't get here in time. Dragging your heels all the way. Good-for-nothing watch turned you into a nigger-lover overnight. I'll teach you a lesson when we get home. One you won't soon forget."

By the time he sat up, the woods were quiet, the men were gone, and a fish was tugging at his line. He flopped the bullhead on the bank. Carefully avoiding its horns, he gently worked the hook free, coiled the line and put it in his pocket, and holding the fish by the gills, climbed slowly down the stony bank.

He chose the biggest rock he could lift. He held it high until his arms shook; then he smashed at the fish's head—again and again and again and again.

The sun was tingeing the treetops before he moved on down the creek. At a shallow bend, he washed the blood from his hands and the tears from his cheeks. From his pocket he pulled the slingshot, dropped it into the water, turned, and walked back through the woods.

*   *   *

Walking the tracks was hard, the railroad ties spaced so far apart, Rap had to hop from one to the other or step on one, then down into the cinders, and up again on to the wood. He tried counting the ties between telegraph poles that fringed the track, but the numbers never came out the same.

When the rails cut across an open meadow, he moved down the embankment and walked in its shadow. He tried not to think why he felt safer there and fixed his mind on Athabasca.

Lacey Jackson told him once if he'd put his ear down to the rails he could hear trains hundreds and hundreds of miles away. He tried it, but he didn't hear anything except a swarm of gnats buzzing over his head. He never believed Lacey anyway.

He squinted up at the sun. He wasn't hungry. He wasn't even thirsty, but the back of his legs ached as if he'd been climbing High Hill.

He lay down beside the embankment to rest. He felt the sound before he heard it. A train! Coming down the track behind him. He stood up as close to the tracks as he dared and waited, his heart pumping in his throat.

He'd seen trains come into the Clearview depot and he'd been riding a train since what seemed forever, but standing right beside the rails with a big black engine blowing out smoke bearing right down on him was something else. He waved both arms as the freight roared by, the windowless cars blurring into smudges of red and yellow and brown as they zipped past. An arm waved back at him as the caboose swerved down the track.

Slowly he trudged on. It seemed as if he had been walking forever and staring up the tracks that drew together until they were just one line ahead of him. He had no idea how far he'd walked or how long, but the higher the sun rose the sleepier he got. After a while he felt as if he were walking and dreaming at the same time, because way, way up ahead, he thought he saw something moving toward him, no bigger than a flea.

He shook his head and shaded his eyes and squinted. As it came closer, he could tell it was a person. A woman. With a basket! And a flowered hat!

"Aunt Spicy!" he screamed and ran so fast he didn't have any trouble leaping from tie to tie.

She stood waiting for him, basket on the ground, arms opened wide, and when he ran up to her, she hugged him so tight he almost lost what was left of his breath.

"Boy." Aunt Spicy's voice was muffled. "I swear, you be the death of me!" Then she laughed. "Not quite yet, now we've found each other."

Rap, his head buried against her shoulder, thought she smelled sweeter than all the flowers in Oklahoma.

"How we going to get to Athabasca, Aunt Spicy? They go on without us?"

"They waiting a few towns up the line. Come on, now. We walk back to this station up here. We catch another train and it take us to our folks."

"But you tired, Aunt Spicy. Walking all this way back for me."

"There's feet, honey, and there's nerves. I been walking on my nerves."

Aunt Spicy stooped to pick up the basket. Rap gently pushed her hand away. "I carry it."

The next train through was a freight. He and

Spicy sat in the caboose, and just when he was thinking of all the things he was going to tell Cassie about caboose-riding, he yawned and rested his head in Aunt Spicy's lap. Before he dropped off to sleep he thought of telling Aunt Spicy about the coon hunters, but he decided he didn't want her to know things like that could happen.

THIRTEEN

"**Y**ou sleep your way clean out of Iowa. It almost noon."

Waking up was bad enough, but waking with a voice shouting right in his ear was enough to spoil what was left of the rest of the morning.

Rap sat up. "Where we be?"

"Place called Minnesota," Cody said in Cassie's best Mrs. Crumpton voice. "Your Aunt Spicy wallop you good?" she asked, wriggling into the seat beside him.

"She don't ever wallop me . . . no more . . . since I grow up. What you doing here?"

"Cassie, she still sick with her burning-bug. Aunt Spicy tell me come here and keep you company." Cody looked around as if to see if anybody was listening, leaned closer, and cupped her hand by Rap's ear. "What you do in them woods?"

Rap looked out the window. It was a different world now: one blue patch of water after another with pines and funny-looking white-barked trees growing in clumps like bunches of flowers.

"I say," Cody jabbed him, "what you do out there all that time?"

118

He let his mouth make the words and tried not to remember. "Built me a fire. Walked up the tracks."

"Too bad you not here for the excitement when they found you was gone. Your Aunt Spicy, she pull a handle. Stop whole train. People just about bounce out of their seats. She make them open the door and she jump off. Reverend Sneed, he couldn't even stop her. She just say, 'You wait at next place. We catch up.' "

Without Cassie, Cody was a talking newspaper.

"I get walloped if I get lost. How come you get lost and everybody glad to see you?"

"Don't know. But I not getting off this train ever again 'til we get to Athabasca!"

Cody "kept company," chattering away until Aunt Spicy sent her back to her mother. The sun was going down. Lakes, trees, and birds disappeared, and houses, factories, and warehouses surrounded them.

They coasted almost silently, weaving through a maze of tracks, and ground to a stop inside a huge, domed station that could have been a castle straight out of one of Mrs. Crumpton's books. Other trains crowded the tracks, with bells clanging and engines puffing, and all sorts of people rushed around through the steam. Colored men in red jackets and caps pushed and pulled carts full of luggage. All the other faces were as white as the steam that billowed around them.

"Whole world white," Rap said.

"Nothing to be afraid of," Aunt Spicy answered. "We just switching tracks."

Slowly the train moved back, threading to a stop between empty freight cars on one side and coal cars heaped full on the other. Like a giant sigh, steam gushed from the engine and everything was quiet.

"How come we stopping here?" Rap peered out into the darkness.

"We be in St. Paul. They want us out of the way," Spicy said with a funny twist to the corner of her mouth. "We ain't going anywhere tonight, but we be long gone by tomorrow afternoon."

Aunt Spicy was wrong. It was three days before they left St. Paul.

Rap knew something wasn't right when Reverend Sneed walked into the car the next morning, his face serious. He stooped over and talked real quiet to Mrs. Sneed; then he slowly straightened up, wiping his face with his handkerchief.

"I got some good news. I got some bad news. Good news is another trainload of folks left Clearview for Athabasca and they not far behind us. Bad news is seems like Canada sending down an immigration man to inspect us before they'll let us cross the border. They made up some new rules. Head of the family has to have fifty dollars to show the man. And we all got to have physical examination by one of their doctors to make sure we all healthy. What they'd like to do is make up an excuse to send us all packing back to Oklahoma, but we not going to be discouraged."

"What this doctor do?" Rap turned to Spicy. "Thought doctors was for dying."

"Probably supposed to keep us from where we going. Nothing to be afraid of. He just take your temperature. Poke around. Look at your teeth. Listen to your heart."

"What about Cassie? She sick. She won't fit in no suitcase."

"What you talking about?"

"Reverend Sneed say if we be sick they pack us back to Clearview."

"Ain't nobody packing Cassie Mapp anywhere. We think of something. She getting better, but she ain't *got* yet. We figure out something before this inspection take place. Far as immigration man know, ain't no sick people on this train."

Reverend Sneed went on. "They'll be starting the inspection this afternoon. This car go first. Until they come for us, we all got to stay right here. Now I go tell the next car." He walked down the aisle, not looking at anyone, still wiping his face with the limp white handkerchief.

Aunt Spicy sat very quiet, staring at the seat ahead. With a jerk, she stood up. "You sit. I go talk."

Rap sat. A hot dry summer wind swept across the cindered tracks, blowing gritty dust through the open window. The midday sun glared against the faded red of the freight cars.

A man walked down the tracks, peered into an empty boxcar, hoisted himself up, and sat. He reached into a paper bag, pulled out an apple, and bit into it. Chewing, he looked around, his eyes following the length of the Athabasca train, then back to Rap.

"Looks like your engine ain't going any faster than mine, son."

Rap wasn't sure if he was supposed to answer or not.

"How long you been sitting there?"

"Since last night."

The man looked up and down the track as if he were expecting somebody. "That'd be too long for me. Train doesn't go, I hop another."

"What if it's not going the right place?"

"Place doesn't matter. Just the going."

"Don't you want to get somewhere?" Rap leaned farther out the window, resting his elbows on the window ledge.

"Far as I'm concerned, anywhere is somewhere." The man chewed out a last bit of apple and tossed the core down on the track.

"You waiting to be inspected too?"

"Inspected?" The man wiped his mouth against his coat sleeve. "Been suspected. Respected, once maybe. Rejected plenty, but can't say I've ever been inspected." He reached into his paper sack again and pulled out another apple. "Here. Catch."

Rap caught the apple.

"Got good hands, boy."

Rap's apple was sweet and juicy. "You got a name?"

"Several." The man rubbed his nose against the back of his hand. "Nigger Joe. Naphead. Boy. When my hair gets gray it'll be Uncle."

"They ain't nice names."

"No. Not my real name either. I'm nobody. Easier that way."

Rap leaned farther out the window. Far up ahead, an engineer jumped down and started walking between the trains. Rap glanced back at the boxcar, but the man-with-all-the-names was gone.

"Hey, you, boy," the trainman shouted up to Rap. "Don't you know no better than to throw your apple cores all over the place?"

"Yes, sir," Rap answered, inching back out of the window.

Later that afternoon Aunt Spicy came down the aisle, a towel in one hand and a wet washcloth in the other. "We got to go now for our inspection. Wipe off your face and hands and remember to do just as the man tells you. Us women be in one place. You men in another."

"Follow me," Reverend Sneed called out and everybody obeyed, forming a line that stretched from the engine almost back to the caboose.

"You keep close, Rap." Spicy turned and started back to the empty train. "I catch up with you."

"You forget something?"

"No," Spicy answered without turning her head. "Got one more thing to tidy up."

Folks wore their best clothes, men in suits and neckties and women in Sunday dresses. Reverend Sneed led them out between the trains, across a whole acre of tracks, just like Moses crossing the desert, and up to the door of a building, twenty times bigger than the Clearview schoolhouse.

"Go in by families," Reverend Sneed directed. "About ten or so at a time."

Two men in uniforms with rows of gold buttons stood at the door writing down the names of everyone who passed through.

"Can I get a picture, Daddy?" A man with a camera stuck up on wooden legs motioned toward Reverend Sneed. "Gather some of your young ones around. Here, you Auntie, step in there behind him."

"My name is William Sneed," the reverend said

in his soft, end-of-the-prayer voice. "Why do you want a picture of us?"

"You're news. Going to be right on the front page of the *St. Paul Pioneer* tonight. Now eight or nine of you little tykes crowd in close." The man's head disappeared under a black cloth. "Look right at the camera now, and show me those white teeth."

Rap stood up straight and tall. There was an explosion like lightning and a cloud of white smoke drifted up into the air.

Aunt Spicy hurried up beside him. "What you blinking for, boy? Got something in your eye?"

"Got my picture took. Going to be in the newspaper." His eyes, even when he closed them, still shot out flashes of white.

"Hope you held your head up. But come now. Our lines moving up. Mind you do just as the white doctor say. Don't talk less they ask you a question."

Aunt Spicy didn't have to tell him. When he got in with that white doctor he'd just close off his mouth, close off his ears, close off his eyes, close off his thinking, close off everything. Rap Davis not be at home to no white man.

Rap "yes-sirred" and "no-sirred" all the way through the poking and prodding and peering and punching.

"Looks like one good, healthy boy," the doctor said, placing a cold silver circle just below Rap's ribs and listening with two black things in his ears that looked like a sling shot. "Your mammy must have brought you up on fried chicken and watermelon."

"No, sir."

"She didn't?" He smiled down at Rap.

"No, sir. Don't have no mammy. Have an Aunt Spicy."

"Oh. I see." The doctor peered into Rap's ears.

"So you're all thinking of going clear up to Athabasca. You know what I heard?"

"No, sir."

"Heard you could pick a snowflake up there, take it inside, melt it, and you'd have enough drinking water for ten days."

"Yes, sir."

"And I heard one old lumberjack say he saw a whole wagon load of you niggers from down south picking snow for three hours before someone told you it wasn't cotton." The doctor laughed so hard he forgot to look in Rap's other ear. Rap wasn't sure what the man was looking for, but whatever it was he must have found it because he went on to Rap's teeth.

"All right. Put your clothes back on," the doctor ordered. "This one's okay," he called up to another man who wrote down something on a big tablet, his left hand curling over the page upside down. He would never have passed Mrs. Crumpton's penmanship class.

Aunt Spicy was waiting for him at the table by the door.

"That over and done with, honey. Wasn't too bad, was it?"

"No. Did you pass, Aunt Spicy?"

"Guess so. Doctor told me I was running a little fever, but I told him if that was all I was running, he was lucky 'cause I'd been running all my life. What'd the doctor tell you?"

"He tried to make jokes, but they weren't very funny. He called us niggers."

"That's one big reason we going to Athabasca."
Spicy's eyes flashed. "We going where we never
have to hear that word out of a white mouth again."

Another uniformed man stopped them at the
door. "Just one more thing, Auntie. We need proof
that you have enough money to take care of yourself and the boy in Canada. Do you have the re-
quired fifty dollars?"

Aunt Spicy dug down inside the collar of her
dress and pulled out a tiny green square. Carefully
she unfolded the bill and held it out for the man to
see. "That ain't enough, got more where that come
from."

Rap watched the red creep up the man's face.
He marked on his paper, tipped his hat, and said,
"That's all I need to see."

"They ain't so bad," Aunt Spicy said as they
walked back to the train, "one at a time."

Rap wasn't sure whether she was talking about
inspection or inspectors.

"What we do next?"

"Get back in the car and wait 'til the man comes
through and checks us off again," Aunt Spicy said
as they hurried toward the train. "Won't take long."

Rap slid in next to the window. Aunt Spicy sat
down with a sigh, took off her flowered hat, and
fanned herself. "Now," she said in a low whisper,
"when this next man come through, you sit still.
Don't move a muscle. And don't go hankering for
something to eat 'cause we not going to get anything out 'til we're clean through with this inspection business."

The man with the red neck who had looked at
Aunt Spicy's money came slowly down the aisle,

stopping at each seat and writing down more things on his big tablet.

"Remember now," Aunt Spicy warned again. "Sit still."

Rap felt something crawling on his bare ankles just where his pants left off. He reached down and scratched and pulled up his sock.

The man was closer now, talking to Mrs. Sneed. Rap tried to sit still as Aunt Spicy had told him, but there was a sharp nip, like a bee sting, up higher now, just below his knee. He pulled up his leg and rubbed the spot.

"What's the matter with you, boy? Didn't I tell you sit still?"

"Something biting me."

Aunt Spicy reached down and shoved her basket hard against the bottom of the seat. When she straightened up, the man was standing over her.

"Spicy Davis and Anson J. Those the right names?"

Rap felt the tickling again, starting at his ankle now and moving up to his knee and down again. It was no bee. It was no fly. It was somebody's fingers!

"Them the right names," Spicy replied as the man moved on.

"Aunt Spicy," Rap whispered. "Somebody under my seat."

" 'Course there be. We hiding our light under a bushel, just like the Good Book say."

Spicy waited until the man left. "Now, scoot your legs up there on the seat out of the way." She stood up, set the basket in the aisle, and pulled out the blanket and pillow from under the seat. "All right. Come out now."

A rumpled and dusty Cassie Mapp unfolded herself.

"Don't you have no sense, girl?" Aunt Spicy scolded. "You want them inspection men find you and send you back to Oklahoma? Laying down there tickling this boy when the man standing right over us."

"Rap had his big old foot right in my face."

"You not sick," Aunt Spicy said trying not to smile. "But it ain't no time to take chances."

"Knew all the time it was you," Rap said as Cassie snuggled down in the seat between them.

"Soon's all the inspection men leave, you hike back to your own car, Cassie. And, Rap . . ." Spicy sank back into the seat. "You go out and look around a bit. We still have to get our railroad certificates from Canada, so we may be here 'til tomorrow. Me, I'm tuckered. I'm going to have me a nap."

FOURTEEN

The Athabasca train still stretched along the siding, squeezed in next to the freight. Rap walked along, looking into the empty boxcars. He had seen enough of St. Paul and trains and tracks and cinders and depots. He was tired of Cassie and Cody and Mrs. Sneed and Reverend Sneed and all the other Clearview folks he had to see every day.

He had almost run out of freight cars to look at when two hands grabbed him under the arms from behind, his feet left the ground, and he was sitting, legs dangling, in the open door of a boxcar. The man-with-all-the-names swung himself up beside Rap.

"Railroad yard's no place to wander around alone. More than one kid your size has up and disappeared in broad daylight."

If the man's clothes hadn't been so shabby, he might have been one of the Clearview folks.

"You have a name, boy?"

"Anson J. Davis. You got a real name?"

"You don't like my others?"

"No, sir."

"All right, Mr. Davis. Call me Frederick Douglass."

Rap's mouth dropped open. If this was Mrs. Crumpton's Frederick Douglass, he must be almost a hundred years old.

"Keep your mouth open like that, boy, you'll be swallowing a fly. I'm not *that* Frederick Douglass. There's more than one of us. Call me Fred." The man hoisted himself up beside Rap.

"How come you still here?"

"Everybody's got to be someplace."

"Where you live?"

"In there." The man motioned behind him.

There was nothing inside the boxcar except a couple of ragged quilts rolled up in a corner.

"Not much there, I know." Fred leaned out and looked up and down the tracks. "Just the necessities."

"You looking for somebody?"

"My friend. He's out rounding up food. We take turns, pushing a broom, toting boxes. Work long enough for a loaf of bread or a hunk of cheese."

"Don't you get tired of trains?"

"Thing about trains, boy, unless they're stopped, they're always moving. And when they're moving nothing stays the same. Nothing to hold you back or hold you down. One day you wake up in the mountains. Next day in the middle of Texas. And you don't have to be part of nothing. Only problem—railroad detectives."

"What's that?"

"Bad news. Not their fault. Just their job. They come around and roust us out. Figure we ought to be buying passenger tickets instead of using their empty space. If folks'd get along without money like we do, the world'd be a whole lot better off."

"That one of them men?" Rap pointed down the track.

"Naw. That's Tiny. Friend I told you about."

A man, bigger than Jesse Creek and both Smolletts put together, lumbered down the track, his shaggy red hair and beard almost covering his face, a newspaper-wrapped bundle in one hand.

"Can't be your friend. He white."

"So he is. He can't help it. Born that way."

Rap was ready to jump down and run back to his own train, but the man was standing in front of them handing the bundle up to Fred.

"Looks like we already got something to eat." He pointed at Rap.

"Don't pay any attention to Tiny, son. He's not half as mean as he looks."

"What you two doing sitting out here like you're on your own front porch? Dicks'll get you." Tiny pulled himself into the car and sprawled just inside the door. "Hand me the grub, Fred." He unwrapped the bundle, set a loaf of bread on the floor and held up a ring of bologna and sniffed. "Think we better eat this 'fore it dies. Want some, kid?"

Rap shook his head.

Tiny pulled out a knife almost as big as Rap's arm and holding the meat as if it were a willow branch sliced off a chunk.

"Where'd you find the kid?" Tiny mumbled, his mouth full.

"Belongs to the train 'longside."

"A bunch of them's got their pictures in the

paper." Tiny shoved the crumpled newspaper across to Fred.

"I be right in front." Rap leaned over and pointed. Aunt Spicy would be so proud. Here he was, not even up to Athabasca yet, and he was already somebody with his picture on the front page of the St. Paul paper.

Fred looked at the picture then read the words. "Daddy Sneed, the bearded father, and his family are shown en route to their promised land in Alberta." Fred looked up at Rap. "Quite a family you got there."

"That paper so dumb!" Rap looked at the words again. "Reverend Sneed, he not nobody's daddy. We ain't no family. That's Mrs. Smollet, the Irby twins, Elsie and Albert Ransom, Laveda Brody and beside her is Baby Mapp. We don't even look alike!"

"Some folks is blind." Tiny chewed noisily.

"Some folks is *color* blind." Fred handed the newspaper to Rap. "Can you read, son? What else do they have to say?"

Rap wasn't sure he wanted to read any more, but he glanced at the column of print next to the picture.

"What's the matter? Words too hard for you?" Fred laughed.

"They not hard," Rap said. Something sour crept up the back of his throat. "They be easy to understand. They say COLORED TRAIN NOT WANTED IN CANADA."

Tiny wiped his mouth. "That ain't news, is it, Fred?"

Rap watched Fred laugh. It was like waves that started some where down at his feet and went all the way up until they busted out of his mouth, but his eyes weren't even smiling. "Why you think I ride these trains? Inside a boxcar everybody's same color."

"What you want to go way up north for anyway?" Tiny asked.

"Everything free."

"Free, huh? Fred, maybe we'd better go too. Closest to heaven we'll ever get."

Fred stood up, stretched, and jumped down on to the track. "Not me. Right now, heaven's California. That's where this freight's going. Want to come along, son?"

"No sir," Rap answered. "Aunt Spicy need me."

"Maybe you take my knife. Might need it up there." Tiny wiped the blade on the side of his pants.

"I not scared. Got my grandpa's knife." Rap pulled it from his pocket.

"Put that back!" Fred's voice was a low growl. "I'll tell you two things to remember. Never take out a knife unless you mean to use it. And don't empty your pockets in front of strangers."

"Yeah," Tiny added. "Not everyone's honest and upstanding like us."

"Rap! Rap Davis! Where you be?" He heard Cody's scream before he saw her come running around the end of the freight.

Rap jumped down from the boxcar.

"What you doing in that place? You on the wrong train." Cody tugged at his arm. "Mrs. Sneed she say you come right now! Aunt Spicy sick . . . been sick all over everything!"

Forgetting all about Fred and Tiny, Rap ran.

Aunt Spicy didn't look sick, stretched out across the seat. She looked as if she were sleeping. He sat

down across the aisle, pulled his knees up to his
chin, and huddled into the corner. He wished he'd
never seen that dumb newspaper, and he'd sure be
glad when the train started moving again.

Spicy stirred. "That you, honey?"

"Yes, ma'am."

"What you doing all scrunched up over there?"

"I thinking about St. Paul. He a good man, wasn't
he?"

" 'Deed he was."

"Wrote all those letters and books and stuff in
the Bible?"

"Yes, he did."

"Was they all true?"

" 'Course they was."

"This St. Paul we're in . . . don't have much to
do with that one, does it?"

"Just named after, Rap. Just named after . . .
like you named after your mama and your daddy—"
Aunt Spicy stopped and rubbed her forehead.

"My daddy?"

She pulled herself up on one elbow. "Rap, honey.
I feeling poorly, somehow. We talk about things
some other time. Maybe you fetch me a drink, I
feel better."

Rap brought the water, and when he handed her
the cup, her fingers were hot like burning coals.

"You got Cassie's bug?"

"If I do, I squash him. Be all right soon as we
start moving again. We keep an eye on each other."
She lay back and covered her face with the quilt.

Late that night, long after Fred and Tiny's freight
had left, the Athabasca train pulled out of St. Paul.

FIFTEEN

No one stopped them at the Canadian border. Days and nights dragged on as the train lumbered north through empty land and around lakes fringed with pine.

Aunt Spicy didn't look out the window much, just had him fetching her water and keeping a cloth cool for her forehead. She looked so tiny, curled up in the seat, all the rich color faded from her face, and when she opened her eyes, they were clouded and blurred as if she were not even seeing what she was looking at.

One night late, Mrs. Sneed put her hand on Rap's shoulder and whispered, "Honey. Your Aunt Spicy take a turn for the worse. We move her."

"Where you take her?"

"Back to the caboose. She rest better there."

"I go with her." Rap sat up. "She not go alone."

"She not be alone." Mrs. Sneed sat down beside him. "I look in on her."

"I stay with her." He grabbed up his pillow and blanket.

The caboose was like a little house on wheels with a stove, table, two cots, and steps leading up to a tiny room full of windows. Aunt Spicy lay on one cot. Rap sat beside her at the table until he got so sleepy he had to lie down.

Mrs. Sneed woke him in the early dawn. "You go back to the next car. Get in with Cassie and Cody 'til I come for you."

The inside of the train was dark, and rain splattered against the windows. He snuggled into the seat beside Cassie and Cody, tucking his blanket around him.

"You taking too much room," Cody complained. "Got your old elbow in my rib."

"You hush now," Cassie warned. "You know Mama say we got to be nice to Rap 'cause of his Aunt Spicy."

"Nothing wrong with Aunt Spicy." Rap sat up.

"Mama say she gonna—"

"Shut your mouth, Cody. You not supposed to tell."

"Tell what?" Rap sat up straighter.

Cody wriggled out of her blanket. "Your Aunt Spicy burning up. Her skin so hot, Mama say, it just peel off. And if fever don't stop she going to die right here on train before we ever get Athabasca."

"Cody Mapp! I'm gonna tell Mama on you. You just wait. She whop your bottom so hard you never sit down again. Spend rest of your life standing up."

"My Aunt Spicy not going to die!" Rap almost shouted.

She couldn't die. If the fever was peeling off her skin, she'd just shed it like that old snake and crawl right out and grow herself a new one.

"No bug going to hurt Aunt Spicy." Rap's throat was dry.

"Can't see them kinds of bug," Cassie whispered. "They germs. Fly around waiting for someone to come along."

"Aunt Spicy not got bugs." Rap's voice shook. "Don't want to talk no more." He pulled the blanket over his head and closed his eyes against the darkness.

"You girls run back to your mama now." Mrs. Sneed was leaning over the seat. "I give Rap some breakfast and then he go back to his Aunt Spicy."

"She better now?"

"Ain't no better." Mrs. Sneed rolled up his blanket. "But she asking for you."

Spicy lay on the cot, her eyes closed.

"Aunt Spicy," Rap whispered. "You all right now?"

She didn't answer. Then her hand moved and she clasped her fingers around his. Her skin was clammy and cold. Her eyes opened. "Some things I got to say to you." She sounded as if she'd been running.

"Don't have to say them now."

"Got to. Ain't been fair with you, honey. Never told you everything." She closed her eyes, and when she opened them again her voice was stronger. "Remember I told you Josie and me and your mama stopped at Lulu's house. She be Dan Creek's wife and their boy was Jesse."

Aunt Spicy was telling the same old story, but this time with names. He sat down on the floor beside her cot.

"Your mama, pretty she was and smart."

"Smart as Mrs. Crumpton?"

"Your mama, Ann, she born knowing. Grew up.

Married a good boy. He just poured all his love into her, so's when she die, he couldn't find no more love to give nobody."

"Did I make her die?"

"No, honey. She got the fever."

"My daddy get the fever too and die?"

"Get the running fever. Run out of the grave-yard that day and kept running."

"Didn't he like me?"

Aunt Spicy paused so long, Rap thought she was asleep. Then she reached for his hand again. "He didn't even know you. Your daddy one mixed-up man. Mad at the world for your mama's dying. So we raised you, Josie and me. Raised you good. You going to be somebody."

"My daddy. He be somebody?"

"Don't know. Have to wait and see."

Wait and see! How could they wait and see when his daddy past and gone?

"I hear your thinking, honey. I tired from pulling thistles from my head. We talk some more later."

All morning the train moved slowly through the wilderness of pine and brush and log and marsh, the caboose swinging from side to side.

"What it look like out there now?" Aunt Spicy didn't open her eyes.

"Nothing but trees." Rap stared out the window.

"No mind. There be a spot big enough for us."

"I was scared when you was sleeping." The words came out from the top of his throat.

"Tell you true, honey, I scared too. I keep floating away like smoke, so far away I can't call you. Look down and see this train smaller than a line of ants, moving up to Athabasca, and you all alone. That's why I keep coming back."

"Your head hurt? Still full of thistles?"

"One big thistle left. Rap, I ain't never told you no lies. Just never told you all the truth. See, honey, one big reason we leave Clearview, I didn't want you to ever be afraid or mad or hurt the ways I was when I grew up. But bigger reason . . . I 'fraid I lose you."

"What you mean?"

"Should have told you long time ago." Her words were no more than a whisper. "You got more relatives than just me. Old Dan Creek . . . he your grandpa."

"My grandpa?" His head whirled as if he were wound up in a swing and the rope untwisting so fast he couldn't see. "My Granny Josie married Dan Creek?"

"Your mama marry Dan Creek's boy."

"You mean . . . ?" The whirling stopped as if Cassie Mapp had grabbed the swing rope. "You mean . . . Jesse Creek . . ."

Spicy closed her eyes as if she were saying a prayer. "He . . . your daddy."

His daddy! The words sucked the breath clean out of him. A daddy? He'd never thought much about *not* having one. Lacey Jackson had one, of course, but Lacey had everything. He hadn't thought much about *having* a daddy, either. He didn't need one. And Jesse Creek, he didn't even look like a daddy.

Aunt Spicy's head jiggled in rhythm to the clicking and swaying of the train while shadows flew past the window.

"Aunt Spicy." Rap touched her hand. "You asleep?"

"Just resting my eyes."

"My name A. J. Creek, then?"

"Your name Anson Jesse Creek."

The name didn't sound right.

"That Jesse Creek big."

" 'Deed he is."

"When I be somebody, I'll have to be a *big* somebody, won't I?"

Spicy reached over the touched his cheek. "You going to be the biggest somebody anybody's ever seen," she whispered.

"But Aunt Spicy . . ."

"Yes, honey."

"If you don't mind, I think I just stay A. J. Davis."

Once, sometime in the night, he woke and thought he was alone; then he heard Aunt Spicy breathing, and he went back to sleep.

When he woke again, two shadows stood by Aunt Spicy's cot. He knuckled the sleep from his eyes and sat up.

"Anson, boy." Reverend Sneed's preaching voice rumbled through the dark. "Your Aunt Spicy she just . . . she just shuffled off her mortal coil."

Rap didn't understand. Aunt Spicy didn't have no mortal coil, and she'd always taught him not to shuffle.

But when Mrs. Sneed smothered him in her big arms, he did understand. When the train stopped in the dark dawn and they took Aunt Spicy away, he understood, and he understood when the train moved again, leaving Aunt Spicy's grave behind.

*   *   *

"Your Aunt Spicy, she gone to her own Athabasca," they said. "She safe in Beulah Land. She feel no pain or sorrow."

The words drifted past.

They told him he could be Anson J. Sneed. They told him he could be Anson J. Mapp. They told him he could stay Anson J. Davis.

He wanted to tell them Anson J. Davis past and gone, high-as-sky-forever gone. He be nobody.

He ate. He didn't taste. He listened. He didn't hear. He talked. He didn't think. He didn't smile until Cassie and Cody Mapp came parading down the aisle one day, taking such little steps, Rap thought they'd trip over their feet.

"How come you walking like that?"

"We practicing being ladies. Athabasca ladies. And we know something . . ."

Cody finished the sentence, "That you don't know."

"What's that?" Rap said before he could stop himself.

"W-w-well-ll," Cassie drew out the word as long as her breath lasted.

"Reverend Sneed, he say," Cody interrupted, "we almost to Athabasca."

"Let me tell him, Cody. Reverend Sneed say other train from Clearview smack dab behind us."

Rap looked out the window. Almost to Athabasca! Trees and brush grew so close together he'd have to chop a place to stand when he got off the train.

"And Mama say," Cassie went on, "Athabasca be *our* place. We don't *never* go 'round back for nobody."

Aunt Spicy had said he'd never have to be afraid or hate or hurt or be hurt. She was wrong! "Afraid" was coon hunters in the woods. "Hate" was a smashed fish in the woods. "Hurt" was her grave back somewhere in Canada.

He had learned all that by himself.

SIXTEEN

"**W**e're here! We're here!" Reverend Sneed shouted as he hurried through the car. "Athabasca at last!"

Rap was ready, dressed in his Sunday shirt and trousers. Beside him on the seat was Aunt Spicy's basket of necessities, empty now except for her flowered hat.

The surrounding woods were heavy with shadows as he stepped down from the train, but the air was fresh and clean like water from Dan Creek's spring. Everybody was shouting and laughing and hugging someone, and Reverend Sneed and Mrs. Sneed were hugging everyone. Rap didn't want any part of the hugging. He walked down the length of the train, past the freight cars, weaving around boxes and crates and dodging folks unloading their belongings, and stopped beside the engine. Prickles ran up the back of his neck. There were no railroad tracks left! They stopped, as if Athabasca were the end of the world.

A narrow lane led across a log bridge to a scattering of unpainted houses clinging to a low hillside. In the other direction, ruts disappeared into a valley of dark timber. Athabasca! The word sounded a whole lot better than the place looked.

"Hey, Rap!"

He hid Aunt Spicy's basket behind the wheels of the engine.

"What you doing?" Cassie and Cody ran toward him, not a bit like Athabasca ladies.

"Got some things to tidy up," he said, remembering Aunt Spicy's words in St. Paul.

"Reverend Sneed say the other train coming in any minute now. You coming with us?"

"I got something to do."

"You miss everything." Cassie smoothed out the wrinkles in her skirt. "Cody and me going to be up in front hollering, 'Welcome to Athabasca.' "

"Seen enough trains," Rap mumbled. "I hear it whistle when it comes."

"But we going to be first."

"We be first," Cody repeated with a series of nods.

"Don't care." Rap turned away.

"Don't care. Don't care," Cassie chanted, twisting her shoulders with each word. "Come on, Cody. We go ourself. Rap Davis no fun, anyway."

Rap waited until they disappeared into the crowd; then he picked up the basket and started toward the timber. Trees grew thick and straight, tall, bare trunks bushing out into black green branches that cut out the sun. A gray dust swirled up like dirty fog with each step. He walked until he could no longer hear voices; then he stopped and looked around. The train whistled from the distance.

One tree stood off by itself, branches fanning out, sunlight filtering through like golden arrows.

At the base of the tree, he set the basket down. The only sounds now were the wind through the leaves and calls from birds whose names he couldn't even guess.

Carefully he lifted the lid of the basket. The flowered hat lay in the bottom. He reached in his pocket for his granddaddy's knife and his other granddaddy's fishline, and without looking, dropped them into the basket. Shutting the lid, he hooked the basket handles over his shoulder and climbed the tree.

It wasn't the Creek way, but there were no caves around to bury in. Besides, Dan told him once that some tribes used trees instead, so the spirits of folks could collect their belongings and right away be part of the sun and rain and wind before they got to their own places. He couldn't let Aunt Spicy go without her hat.

He wove a small branch through the handles of the basket and pushed it back against the trunk until he was sure it would stay. He climbed down and sat, his back pressed against the tree.

A. J. Nobody, that's who he was. Everybody he'd ever known was past and gone. There wasn't any reason to stay here in Athabasca without Aunt Spicy. Some day the train would have to go back south. There weren't any tracks to go ahead. No reason to go back to Oklahoma either. Nothing back there. Dan Creek dead. Jesse Creek didn't want him. If he did, he'd have said something long time ago. Maybe he'd hide in a boxcar and ride back to St. Paul, catch up with Fred and Tiny. No telling, though, if he'd find them.

A. J. Nobody in a nowhere place. No reindeer. No igloos. No Eskimos. No fat fish. Just trees, one after another, all alike, pushing down on him 'til he could hardly breathe.

He saw the boots first, fancy high-heeled cowboy boots with decorations across the toes and running up the sides. A shadow cut off the sun. He raised his eyes slowly, past the big silver belt buckle until he was looking into black eyes, narrowed as if the man were staring straight into the sun.

Jesse Creek stood, hands in pockets, wide-brimmed hat pulled low, his face closed in as if he were hiding somewhere back of his eyes.

Rap opened his mouth, but no words came. Jesse Creek belonged back in Clearview, not up here in Athabasca.

Jesse didn't say anything, either, only stood there looking at Rap as if there weren't anything else to see.

"Aunt Spicy ..." Rap's tongue was thick and heavy. "She ... she ..."

"Mrs. Sneed told me." Jesse's voice sounded different; then it changed back to the one Rap remembered. "I'm not going to eat you, boy. Why you looking at me that way?"

"How you get here?"

"On the other train. Didn't you hear the whistle? Cassie Mapp said you were here. Not hard to follow your tracks." Jesse Creek hadn't moved any closer.

"Why you come?"

" 'Cause you left. And I couldn't let you go." Jesse hunched down on his knees, stared at the ground as if he were looking at a map, then glanced back up. "Your Aunt Spicy keep her promise to me?"

"Don't know nothing about promises."

"She promised she'd tell you."

"She say Dan Creek be my granddaddy."

Jesse nodded slowly.

Rap felt all the things rolled up into one big ball in his stomach—fear and hurt and anger—and something else, too. Something he couldn't name. Something he'd never felt before.

"Why *you* not tell me?"

A muscle in Jesse's jaw tightened, then relaxed. "I promised something too. Promised your granny and Spicy, when I left that time, that you was theirs and I'd never come back and claim you. Hard to understand, maybe. You don't know what it's like when you lose someone you—" He stopped and stood up. "Guess you do understand now, don't you?"

The sound of Jesse's words, the look on his face, made the bad feelings begin to fade, not all at once, but a little around the edges.

"You really be my daddy?"

"If you want me." Jesse took a step toward him. "Don't know how good I'll be. Not had much practice."

"I have to be A. J. Creek, then?"

"If you want to. Got to be somebody. Sometimes it takes a while to find out who."

"Find out here in Athabasca?"

Jesse tipped his hat back from his forehead and bit his lip. "Can stay and homestead. Or go back. Your granddaddy left you his Oklahoma land. And there's still Aunt Spicy's place, if you want it. Plenty of time to decide. We got a lot of catching up to do."

We was Aunt Spicy and Rap. He wasn't sure he wanted to be half a "we" with Jesse Creek.

"Aunt Spicy say you got running fever. She say you not got your boots on the ground."

"Your Aunt Spicy was right . . . once." Rap could hardly hear the words. "Running's done. I promise. What you think?"

Rap looked up into the tree.

"I move it about in my mind," he said, watching the branches sway in the breeze.

"Maybe . . . we go back now and pick up our stuff? You ready?"

Rap stood up, dusted off his best trousers, and looked up at Jesse Creek. "Why not? I all done here."

Together they walked back through the edge of the timber.

"This way, everybody!" Reverend Sneed shouted, his arms stretched high above his head as both trainloads of Clearview folks crowded behind him. "We've found our promised land! And no Jim Crow perching in them trees!"

Rap stopped. He could not move. It was no mistake! Right there beside Reverend Sneed, book in one hand, leather satchel in the other, walked . . . MRS. CRUMPTON!

"Oh, Reverend Sneed!" She dropped her book and satchel. "You were right! I was so wrong!" Her words rang out. "This will be a magnificent place. The land cleared. The grain golden." She looked back at all the Clearview folks as if she were getting ready to assign buckets, then turned and gazed out across the land. "For all of us, an

Amber Valley. However—" She looked straight at Rap. "First we build *the school*."

Rap felt the warmth of Jesse's big hand on his shoulder. "Well, what do you think . . . son?"

"Don't know yet. My mind's unsettled." Rap took a deep breath. "First I got to decide about school and being somebody."

He started toward the train, stopped, and looked back. Jesse Creek hadn't moved to follow him.

"But when I'm bigger, if we go back to Oklahoma some day"—Rap grinned—"maybe I find me a pair of boots like yours."

And It Really Happened . . .

Rap is a part of me, although I grew up in South Carolina, not Oklahoma. Like Rap, I saw bits and pieces of everything. I watched Reedy River flow past and was fascinated by the water because it was headed someplace. I wanted to go, too—where, I wasn't sure. The river had a destiny, maybe my destiny. I knew I was going to *go* some place and *be* somebody. Finally, I did go: Miami, New York, San Juan, Mexico City, Los Angeles, Vancouver, Paris, Clearview, Athabasca.

I first heard about Athabasca while stationed at a radar site in North Dakota in 1958. I learned that my people had thrived in the coldest agricultural region of Canada although books I had been given maintained blacks could not withstand the rigors of cold weather, propaganda used to keep Oklahoma migrants out of Canada between 1910 and 1913. After I survived a winter in North Dakota and two more winters north of Winnipeg, I knew those books were wrong. Eleven years later, I met the people of Athabasca. Now, fourteen years after my first encounter, I have come to know the people and community of Amber Valley well.

From my experiences, documents, and tapes, Hadley Irwin has crafted *I Be Somebody*. My own manuscript, *All That Blood, The Amber Valley Saga*, chronicles the migration from the all-black towns of Oklahoma to the new settlement in Alberta. After the Civil War, my people moved into the "American" frontiers—Indian Territory, Oklahoma Territory, Arizona Territory and border states—searching for a place of refuge from the historic discrimination they had suffered in the Old South. They left their original homes filled with hope for claiming goods and services that were supposed to be the result of hard work, fear of God, and clean, moral living. But as *I Be Somebody* shows, their dreams were deferred until Athabasca.

Most of the characters you have met in this book are composites of real people, but situations were changed to develop the story. Mrs. A. H. Cromwell (Mrs. Crumpton), for example, was a teacher in Amber Valley for more than twenty years. Although the name "Spicy" came from the aunt of one of the white authors, the Aunt Spicy of *I Be Somebody* might have been my mother, who had nothing to do with the trip, but well might have been on that train had she lived in Clearview.

Hadley Irwin and I want to assure you that Rap Davis DID become somebody. And you can too—be somebody.

Dr. Charles C. Irby
Professor of Ethnic and Women's Studies
California State Polytechnic University
Pomona, California